Return to Anoria

the sequel to

The Nelig Stones

by

Sharon Skinner

Brick Cave Media

brickcavebooks.com

Return to Anoria

ISBN: 978-1-938190-59-9

Cover & Internal Illustration Artist: Kyna Tek
www.kyteki.com

Brick Cave Media
brickcavebooks.com

For Buzz

Return to Anoria

SHARON SKINNER

Brick Cave Media
brickcavebooks.com

CHAPTER ONE

Stefani twisted the silver ring on her finger, turning it around and around, until it began to spin on its own. She stared, fascinated, wondering why the friction of the silver band against her finger didn't burn as science said it should. Then she heard someone crying and a voice calling her name.

She stared out at the horizon. Dark shadows covered everything. They slithered and shifted away from her gaze. Each time she tried to focus on a familiar shape, it morphed and melted into nothing.

"Mom?" Stefani called. "Is that you?"

The crying grew to a wail. The sorrow-filled weeping of a woman in distress.

"Mom!" Stefani shouted, her fear rising. "Mom! I'm

sorry! I didn't—"

A high-pitched shriek cut off her words and her hands flew to her ears. She pressed with all her might, but the horrible sound grew louder. Beneath the screaming sound, someone called her name, over and over.

The voice was familiar, and the more she concentrated on it, the clearer it became. As the voice rose, the shrieking faded away.

"Stefani," the voice called. "We...need..."

She knew that voice. Stefani took her hands from her ears, struggling to remember.

A wind rose up, rattling the tree branches, the leaves shushing in the darkness.

"Stefani," the voice called again, and with sudden recognition, Stefani knew the speaker. Laurel Silverbark, the Treemage in Anoria who had helped her and Robbie in their quest for the Nelig Stones.

Laurel was calling out to her. Calling for help.

Stefani spoke into the darkness. "Laurel?" The wind rose up, whipped her hair into her eyes and stung her cheeks. An icy dread took hold of her. Something was wrong. Terribly, terribly wrong. "Laurel!"

"...please...help..." Laurel's voice sounded weak and distant. "...Anoria...the Queen..." The words grew faint, melting away like the fading shadows.

"Laurel!" Stefani cried, reaching out to the darkness. "What's wrong? What can I do?"

"Come," the Treemage's voice was barely a whisper, now. "Come...back."

"How?" Stefani called. "How do we get back?" She ran toward the voice, but it vanished into nothing. "Laurel?" The wind beat at her, driving her back. She leaned against it, pushing herself forward.

She tumbled to the floor and woke with a start.

Familiar shapes loomed in her darkened bedroom. She had to do something. The dreams were getting worse.

She wanted to text Robbie, get him to understand. But it was three o'clock in the morning and he was probably sound asleep.

Unlike her.

She straightened her sheets and blankets and climbed back into bed. She had to convince Robbie how important it was for them to go back. So far, he'd shied away from the idea. He'd even used soccer practice as an excuse.

They couldn't wait any longer. She and Robbie had to find a way to return to Anoria. And they had to do it soon.

CRISO
SOCR

CHAPTER TWO

Robbie peered out the window and cringed as his father's car pulled into the driveway. The driver-side door opened, and his father got out and strode around to the passenger side to hold the door open for his grandfather. Gramps looked like he was lost. Why did they have to bring him here? Why couldn't they let him stay where he was?

Robbie rushed upstairs to his room, so he wouldn't have to greet them when they came inside. Maybe he could pretend to be sick and just stay in his room. But for how long? How long before his grandfather would be able to move into Evening Shadows Retirement Community?

"Robbie!" Dad shouted up the stairs.

Robbie shoved a pillow over his head and tried not to hear his father calling him.

"Robbie, come down and say hello to your grandpa."

"Aw, he don't want anything to do with an old man like me."

Robbie sat up, tense, waiting. It sounded like Gramps remembered him, this time.

"Sure he does, Pop. Come on into the living room and get comfortable. I'll grab us something cold to drink."

Robbie stood by the bedroom door and listened again. Maybe, just maybe, he should go down and see.

He went down the stairs, one slow step at a time, stopping at the bottom landing. He took a breath before stepping into the living room.

Gramps sat in Dad's recliner, but instead of putting his feet up, he leaned forward, staring at his hands. He rubbed his knuckles against the bandages that wrapped around his left hand. "Not right," he said. "Not right to take a man out of his home."

"Gramps?"

"Hmmm?" His grandfather looked up and narrowed his eyes. "Do I know you?" His face wrinkled in confusion.

Robbie felt like he'd been punched.

"It's me, Gramps." He pointed to himself. "Robbie."

"Oh, Robbie." Gramps smiled, but it looked awkward, like he was trying too hard. "Oh, sure. Sure."

"You don't really remember, do you?"

"Course I do." The old man scratched at his chin. "Larry's boy, right?"

"Yes." Robbie nodded, hope allowing him to breathe again. Maybe things would be okay. Maybe, it would be different this time. Not like the time in the park when Gramps had lost it so bad. He'd been so embarrassed for his grandfather that day.

"How's your hand?" Robbie asked.

"My hand?" Gramps looked down at his hands again. "Oh." He shrugged. "That's nothing. Why, with any luck, they'll ship me home for this one." He grinned and waved his hand in the air. "Yup. Might just get me a ticket home." He looked around in confusion.

"But Gramps, you can't live at home anymore. They said you need a different living arrangement. That's why—"

His grandfather shook his head. "That's not right." He stood up and marched across the room. "I need to get home." He grabbed for the doorknob, but the bandages on his hand slipped on the knob and he couldn't get it to turn.

He reached his other hand up and tried to grip the knob in both hands, but he must have bumped the lock button because the door wouldn't budge. "Let me outta here. Let me outta here."

"Gramps," Robbie reached for his grandfather. "Stop. You're going to hurt yourself."

"Don't you tell me what to do. I'm a grown man. I don't need anyone telling me what to do." Gramps kicked at the door, but his foot just bounced off and he sank down onto the floor. "Please," he moaned. "Please, just let me out. I need to go home." Tears ran down his wrinkled face.

Robbie's gut twisted. He didn't know what to do. He didn't know who this man was sitting in a heap in front of him, but it wasn't his grandfather. It couldn't be. His grandfather had been proud and brave. He'd served and fought overseas. He'd saved a man's life. The person in front of him who threw tantrums and whined and cried? That wasn't Gramps. Never Gramps.

Robbie's father came into the living room, carrying two frosty glasses. "Lemonade?"

Robbie shot his father a nasty look. "Lemonade? You think lemonade is going to fix anything?" He pounded up the stairs to his room and slammed the door behind him before throwing himself down onto his bed. How could they bring him here? How? Robbie shoved his head under his pillow.

Maybe, Stefani was right. Maybe they *should* find a way back to Anoria.

He sure didn't want to stick around here, anymore.

CHAPTER THREE

Robbie looked up from his drawing when Stefani entered his uncle's silk-screening shop. "Hey, Stef."

The shop held the sharp odor of ink and cleaning solvents. The clack and whir of the silk-screening machines echoed around the small space, setting up a rhythmic background that Stefani always found hypnotic.

"Hey," she said, slipping off her backpack. "You okay?"

"Sure. Why?"

She unzipped the main pocket, reached in and pulled out a hardbound book. "No reason. You just look kind of . . . not so happy."

"Sheesh. Why does everybody keep bugging me about looking happy?" He took the book from her. "I'm fine, all right?"

"Sorry," she said. "But if you ever need to talk about anything, I'm always available."

"Yup. Got it. Heard you the first twenty times, but this isn't the Teen Line, and I'm not one of your callers. Okay?"

"Okay." Stefani tried not to look as hurt as she felt. It was pretty clear Robbie was in a bad mood, and she didn't feel like getting into a fight with him. Besides, if there was one thing she'd learned talking to other kids about their problems, it was not to push. Oh, well, there goes talking about Anoria, she thought, her heart dropping below her knees. Maybe, she ought to just figure out a way to get there on her own. Only, the thought of going back there without Robbie gave her a sour feeling in her stomach.

"I'm just going to go put this in the back for Uncle Ray." Robbie went out through the doorway at the back of the shop, brushing past as his uncle stepped into the room.

The tall man waited until Robbie was out of earshot before saying, "Don't mind him. He's been in a bad place ever since his grandfather moved in with the family last week." He wiped his hands on an ink-stained rag. "Mr. Peters isn't doing so well living on his own, what with his advancing memory loss and all." He tapped his head with a finger.

"I knew he was getting more forgetful, but Robbie didn't tell me it was bad enough that they had to move him in to their house."

"It's pretty fresh." He reset one of the silk-screening machines to be ready for a new round of printing the next day. He worked while he spoke, switching out the screens, and checking the station alignments. "It's a tough situation, especially for Robbie. He and his dad's dad have always been really close, since Robbie's mom's dad—my dad—died before Robbie was born."

"I guess I hadn't really thought about that," Stefani said.

"Sometimes it takes time for people to process feelings." He glanced toward the back of the printing shop and lowered his voice. "I'm sure he'll talk about it when he's ready."

"Uncle Ray, I put your book on the desk." Robbie said, coming out of the back room.

"Thanks." His uncle removed a screen from its clamps and examined it. "How'd you like the book?" he asked Stefani before setting the screen aside and picking up another one.

"It was great," Stefani said. "I like unicorns."

Robbie flashed her a look.

She shrugged. "I mean, who doesn't like a good unicorn story?"

"Well, that one's a classic. They even made an animated film from it, back when I was a kid. I bet you could rent it on DVD, or stream it, or something."

"That would be fun," Stefani said.

"Why don't you kids head on out. I've got things handled here." Robbie's uncle added the screen to the others leaned against the wall and looked at his watch. "Besides, you're off the clock, Robbie."

"I could stay and help you clean up," Robbie said, sounding hopeful.

His uncle glanced over at Stefani. "I think Stefani needs to get home, and I'm sure her parents would prefer she has someone to walk with."

"Yeah. Yeah. I know. Come on, Stef." Robbie frowned, but grabbed his bag from behind the sales counter and slung it over his shoulder.

Stefani looked from one to the other and picked up her backpack. "Thanks again for the book loan, Mr. Robbins."

"Anytime, kiddo." Robbie's uncle waved them out the door.

Stefani expected the walk home to be filled with silence, but they were hardly out the door and down the street before Robbie blurted out. "I'm ready to go back. Just tell me what we need to do."

CEEG
EGCE

CHAPTER FOUR

It was early morning when Stefani and Robbie arrived at the park. The sun was barely up. The chill air from the night clung to the ground in low-lying pockets.

Robbie shifted his pack higher onto his shoulders where it could ride most comfortably, adjusting it the way their friend Gamdol had showed him during their first trip to Anoria. He pictured Gamdol's bright eyes and quick smile. It would be good to see him again. Gamdol had faced the world with curiosity and bravery, even overcoming his fear of water when it had been necessary. Maybe some of that bravery would rub off on him.

Robbie glanced over at Stefani. They'd had no warning the first time they'd been transported there. It had been an accident and a surprise to both of them. But this time would be different. This time they were purposely going to try to pass through the gate of worlds. Their packs were crammed full of food, camping equipment, and an assortment of extra clothes. "You never know," Stefani had said as they made the list of what to bring. "With time passing so differently there, it could be winter now. We should try to be prepared this time."

They'd met at the light rail station and boarded the eastbound train. Robbie sat in the seat beside her, shifting nervously and looking around at the people near them. Finally, when the car was almost empty, he reached into his pocket and pulled something out, holding it in his fist for a moment. "I have something for you," he said.

"For me?" Stefani asked in surprise.

"Yeah. That is, if you want it." He held up his fist.

Stefani held out her hand, palm up.

Robbie opened his fist and dropped a piece of faceted amethyst the size of a robin's egg into her hand.

"Oh, it's so cool." Stefani held the lavender stone up so it caught the sunlight streaming in through the window.

Robbie gazed at the gemstone for a moment, then turned away and stared out of the window. "It was something we found. My grandpa and me. Long time ago at the gem show."

"Oh, then you should keep it," Stefani said, trying to give the stone back to him.

"No." His voice was tight. "I don't want it. I mean . . . I just thought . . . I figured it's more something that you'd like."

"Thanks," she said as they reached their stop. She slipped the crystal into her jeans pocket and gave him a goofy smile that made his insides feel funny.

"Sure." Robbie focused his attention on the train's doors. "It's not a big deal."

They transferred to the first morning bus that stopped near the zoo. From there, they hiked over to the park and made their way up the trail that led toward Hole-in-the-

Rock. Robbie looked back at Stefani. Hiking up the path behind him, she was bent over under the weight of her pack, and her hair had fallen over her face. He could still see the outline of her chin and the way her lips curved. She had changed a lot in the past half year. They both had. He had grown over four inches taller and was now the captain of the soccer team. Bullies like Freddy didn't bother him, anymore.

Stefani was different now, too. She was friendlier and more relaxed than when they had first met. She was getting along better with her mother most of the time and even trying to help other kids with their problems. When she wasn't putting in hours at the Teen Help Line, she and Robbie spent a lot of time together. She seemed to change a little more every time he saw her.

Stefani raised her head to look up and he quickly turned his eyes back to the trail ahead, nearly tripping in the process. He could feel the heat rising on his neck and hoped she couldn't tell he was blushing.

"Hey," she called out. "You going to go all the way around the park?"

He looked back and realized that he'd walked right past the opening to Hole-in-the-Rock. "I was just checking things out," he shot back quickly.

"Well, since there's no one else in the park, I'm just going to set my stuff down here," she said, sliding her pack off her shoulders and setting it down in the shade next to the big rock formation.

Robbie walked back to where she stood and shrugged off his pack. As he set it down next to hers he realized she had picked the exact spot where they had bumped into one another the first time they'd met. *Well, I bumped into her,* he corrected himself, remembering how he had careened around the corner, running from Freddy. He'd crashed headlong into her and they'd both fallen down. Hard. When he'd gotten back up, everything had changed. Thinking about it now, it seemed like it had happened a really long time ago, and not just six months back. "What now?" he asked.

"I don't really know," she said. "I think it was probably finding the Greatstone that let us open the gates the first time. I mean, I'd been here hundreds of times before that day and nothing like that had ever happened before. The Greatstone, and the writing, I guess," she said. "You know, the strange symbols I told you about." She reached down and brushed her hand over the spot she'd been staring at the day he'd run into her.

Robbie ran his fingers over the rock. It felt cold and hard, but like the many times they'd returned here after their first adventure, there were no symbols and nothing unusual happened when he touched it.

"Maybe we should look around for another strange rock, or something else that's out of place," he suggested, trying to sound hopeful. He didn't really think they would find anything, and he wasn't exactly sure why they should want to. He still worried about what might happen if they really did get the Gate of Worlds open again. How could they be sure they would actually go back to Anoria? It could be like some crazy time-travel thing or a bad Star Trek rerun. If they timed it wrong they could end up somewhere else. Then what? And if they did get back to Anoria, what then? The time difference was so great, everything might have changed completely.

Stefani looked over at him and smiled. Robbie bit his lip. Stefani was right about one thing. If their friends really were in trouble, they should at least try to help them. He began to walk around, searching the ground carefully.

They had become close friends over the past half year. At first, it had been just that, two people who had shared an experience that no one else could understand. It really only made sense, he reminded himself. Who else could they talk to about it besides each other? No one else would believe them.

But now they shared a lot of other things, too. They studied together and Stefani went to almost all of Robbie's soccer games. They'd even started skating together, Robbie on his skate board, Stefani on the inline skates she'd asked for and gotten for her thirteenth birthday. And now, here they were, trying to get back to Anoria together.

"There must be a way back." Stefani faced the rock and ran her hands gently over the surface.

ೞ಼ೞ
ೞ಼ೞ

CHAPTER FIVE

They'd searched for most of the morning, and found nothing. The sun had risen high in the sky, warming the air, but the huge rock formation was still cool to the touch. Robbie continued making his way around the big rock formation, scanning the ground and dragging his fingers along the bumpy surface of the rock.

Stefani's hands were dirty and chafed from poking against the rock every few inches. She sat down in the shade with her back against the outcropping as Robbie came back around from the other side. "I can't find anything unusual," he said. "It's all just ordinary local sand and rock. Nothing special."

"Me either." Frowning, Stefani pulled her pack closer so she could reach one of the water bottles that hung from it.

She took a long drink, then poured a little of the water on her hands. Then, she pulled an orange bandana out of her pocket and dried her hands on it. "I don't understand. I was so sure there was a way in. I felt it. I can still feel it. In my dreams, I saw us back there. It was so clear." She puffed up her cheeks and blew out her breath in frustration.

"Maybe they are just dreams, after all," Robbie said.

"If you didn't believe me in the first place, why are you even here?"

"I'm sorry, Stef. I didn't mean it. I just don't know what else to do. We've been here all morning, and we don't really even know what we're looking for."

"I know," she said. "I'm sorry, too. I didn't mean to snap at you." She took another drink of water.

"Listen," he said, coming over to where she sat. "Maybe we need to look at it differently. Maybe there's a special day we have to be here or something. Or maybe you'll have another dream that will tell us what we need to do. Come on, it's almost noon and I'm starving. Let's go get something to eat." He picked up his pack with one hand and reached out with the other to help her up. Stefani nodded and put her water bottle back in the side pocket. She grabbed the strap of her pack and reached up to take his hand.

As their fingers touched, the sky went dark. Startled, they both let go, and Stefani plopped back down onto the dirt.

Robbie turned quickly and stared out at the forest of Anoria. "Wow!" he said, looking down at his hand as if it had been burned. "I sure didn't expect that."

"Me neither." Stefani stood up. She gazed out at the trees that had replaced the desert landscape of cacti and low brush. Her hand tingled where Robbie had touched her and the silver ring she always wore was warm to her touch.

"Do you suppose...? Could it have been...us?" Robbie asked.

"Maybe. Or us and...last time, the stone...but this

17

time...the ring?" She turned the little band around on her finger, examining it thoughtfully. "Laurel did say it held some kind of magic."

"Well, if it got us here, maybe it can get us home again," Robbie said, reaching out to grab her hand.

"No." She yanked her hand out of reach. "Even if it can, we can't go back now. We just got here."

"I just wanted to test it," Robbie said. "So we'd know. If it does work, we can always come right back."

Stefani hesitated, looking out at the forest. It wasn't the friendly place she recalled. It seemed darker. A lot of the trees looked like they were dead or dormant. Their bare branches scratched at the sky and clawed at one another. Stefani shivered. Before this, all her thoughts had been focused on getting back here, on helping their friends. She hadn't considered the risk they might be taking. But now that they were here, she couldn't ignore the danger. She looked back at Robbie, weighing things in her mind before answering him.

"What if it only works once?" she said quietly. "There's just so much we don't know. What if, after we got home, we couldn't come back here. Ever?"

Robbie frowned. "I guess that's possible."

"Besides," she said, "if King Emrys sent us home once, he should be able to again, right?"

"Sure. If he's still the king," Robbie said, looking around them. "I mean, it's been a half year for us, and when we were here before, weeks passed here in what was a few minutes back in our world. An awful lot of stuff could have changed by now. Just look at the forest." He jutted his chin in the direction of the dark trees. "It sure doesn't look the same."

"Or feel it." Stefani hugged herself. "But we can't just leave without trying to find Laurel. She called to me. She needs us. Now that we're here, we have to try and help her."

Robbie squared his shoulders. "Okay. I'm with you.

What do you think we should do first? It's already late afternoon here, and I doubt we can expect Gamdol to come walking by and find us again."

"I guess not," Stefani replied. "I suppose we could camp here for the night and start out in the morning. It looks like something horrible has happened to the trees around here since our last trip, and I'd rather not go into the forest at night." She peered at the unhealthy-looking trees that marched gloomily from the edge of Hole-in-the-Rock out into the darkening distance.

The ground lurched, and the earth beneath her feet began to vibrate. A rumbling sound came from below, echoed inside Hole-in-the-Rock cavern, and grew louder as the ground shifted and shook harder. Gravel and sand tumbled down the sides of the rock formation.

"Earthquake!" Robbie shouted, bending his knees to keep his balance.

Stefani scanned the area for someplace safe. There was nowhere to go. No doorway to hide in, except the entryway to the cavern where rocks and dirt poured down like rain. "We need to do something," she called, shifting her weight to stay on her feet.

"The forest," Robbie hollered. "Look! The trees aren't moving. It's just the rocks up here."

The ground continued to tremble. More gravel and rocks tumbled down. Stefani lost her balance, falling onto her back, and slid down the side of the rock formation along with the shifting trail of dirt. A large pile of debris slammed into her, ripping her backpack from her grip and taking it over the side.

"Look out!" Robbie grabbed her hand just before she slid off the ledge. Below them her backpack crashed into branches and brush on its way to the forest floor.

She grasped his wrist with her free hand, her feet dangling out over the long drop. She forced herself not to look down.

"Hang on," Robbie told her, stumbling to keep from being swept along with the rocks and dirt that flowed past them and crashed over the edge.

Stefani gritted her teeth and clung to Robbie as the earth bucked beneath them. Dirt and dust pelted her, and she blinked her stinging eyes.

Robbie backed away from the edge, pulling Stefani with him. His feet slipped on loose dirt and gravel.

"Let go, or we'll both fall," Stefani shouted as she felt herself slip farther over the edge.

"No!" Robbie gripped harder and leaned away, digging in his feet.

The ground heaved and Robbie fell backward, his breath whooshing out of him. He gasped. Coughing and choking, he clung to Stefani while they both slipped closer to the edge.

Stefani squeezed her eyes shut and tried to let go, but Robbie tightened his grip. Their eyes met.

"Hang. On." His words huffed out between coughs.

The ground gave a final shudder, then stopped moving.

With Robbie pulling, Stefani managed to kick and wriggle herself back onto the outcropping. She crawled away from the edge and they both collapsed. Clouds of dust filled the air around them.

"You okay?" Robbie asked, coughing.

"I think so. Nothing feels broken or sprained, at least. Just bruised and scratched." Stefani wiped her face. "You?"

"I'm okay. Just a little freaked from us almost being tossed off the ledge like that."

"Yeah." Stefani bit her lower lip. "Thanks, by the way, for not letting go."

"Well, at least now we know holding hands won't send us back." Robbie gave her a half smile.

The back of Stefani's neck grew warm. "Well, I suppose we're going to have to go down into the forest after all," she said, looking up toward the place where the Hole-in-the-Rock cavern used to be. "The doorway to the cavern is completely covered."

Robbie unslung his bottle of water and took a swig, rinsing and spitting. "I guess it's just as well the earthquake happened when it did." He passed the bottle to Stefani.

She rinsed her mouth and took a drink to clear her throat. "Yeah, we could have been trapped inside, if we'd decided to camp in there."

"We also need to recover your backpack before it gets dark." Robbie ran his fingers through his hair trying to dislodge some of the soil and grit stuck there.

"Or before some animal decides to try and eat it."

"Don't say that," Robbie said.

"Sorry. I guess I forgot how dangerous it can be here. So much of it really did seem like a dream before—"

"You mean before the land tried to shake us off as soon as we got back?"

"Yeah." Stefani frowned and handed the water bottle back. "Kind of weird, don't you think?"

"Not any weirder than being transported to a completely different world than our own. Twice now." He took another drink, then re-stowed the bottle. "Let's get going before it tries to get rid of us again." He stood, hoisting his pack and started down the rutted path that led into the gloomy forest.

"I'm right behind you," Stefani said, stepping carefully to keep from slipping on the loose soil. "Better a creepy forest than an angry rock formation."

"I hope you're right," Robbie muttered.

CHAPTER SIX

Slipping and sliding on loose rubble, Stefani and Robbie finally made their way down the side of the rock formation. Picking their way through the scraggly bushes that surrounded it, they forged a path to the area below the ledge. By the time they found Stefani's pack, they were battered, scratched and bruised.

Stefani shook her pack, dumping off the excess dirt and gravel, before hefting the pack onto her back. "I am completely covered in dirt," she grumbled, brushing her hands off on her jeans and raising another cloud of dust.

Robbie took a drink of water and offered his bottle to Stefani. "I have so much dirt up my nose, if I sneezed, mud would come out."

"That's gross," she said, with a small laugh.

Robbie tilted his head to the side. "Yeah, but I made you smile."

Stefani shrugged. "Any idea which way we should go? The last time we were here we had Gamdol to guide us, and I don't really remember which direction we went from here."

"I think we went that way." He pointed off toward an especially dismal-looking part of the forest.

Stefani held her compass in the palm of her hand. "If you're right, we need to go northwest from here." She passed the compass to Robbie, then pushed her hair up off her forehead and tied it back with her bandanna.

"I guess we might as well go as far as we can before it gets dark." Robbie clipped his water bottle onto his belt. "I brought extra batteries for my flashlight, but it'd be better not to use them up if we can help it."

Stefani eyed her scratched up arms. "If we can find an animal track that's heading in the right direction, we won't have to fight the undergrowth so much."

"Yeah, but what are the chances of that?" Robbie stopped to pull away from a thorny bush that had caught his sleeve.

Stefani pushed ahead through the tangle of branches and half-dead vines. Now and then, she checked the compass to make sure they were still headed in the right direction. Or at least what they hoped was the right direction. Once she reached the edge of the forest, she paused, waiting for Robbie to catch up. Now that she stood beneath the skeleton–fingery tips of the outstretched branches, the forest felt even darker and meaner.

Robbie stepped up beside her. "You okay?"

Stefani shrugged. "It's just so..."

"Creepy?" he asked.

"More like...I don't know..."

"Sick." Robbie said it, like he knew without a doubt that's what was wrong.

Stefani shivered. That was exactly it. The forest didn't feel bad as much as suffering. "I think you're right," she said, keeping her voice low. "But what could make an entire forest sick?"

"I don't know," Robbie said, "but it must be something really bad. And why does Laurel need *us*? I mean, she's a Treemage. Seems to me, healing sick trees and plants and stuff would be her business."

Stefani turned the silver ring around and around on her finger and an uneasy feeling crept over her. "Unless whatever is making the trees sick is making her sick, too."

"I still don't know what we're supposed to do about it." Robbie swiped his sleeve across his forehead.

"I don't know either. Or why in my dreams she kept talking about the Queen. How are *we* supposed to help Queen Karissa? I mean, she has a whole army." Stefani took another heading, then shoved the compass back into her pocket. "I guess the only way to find out is to find Laurel."

"I guess you're right, but I don't like the looks of this forest." Robbie shook his head.

"Neither do I," Stefani said. The shadows beneath the dead branches seemed thicker than they should be, like the trees oozed with gloom. Their branches jutted out like crooked fingers. "But, now that we're here, it's not like we have a lot of options." She took a deep breath and exhaled. "Plus, I can't go home until I know why she called to me in my dreams. Not being able to sleep through the night is getting really old. And besides, I really think we should do something to help fix this, if we can."

"Agreed." Robbie glanced back over his shoulder.

Stefani followed his gaze. Behind them, the formation that was Hole-in-the-Rock back home jutted up against the sky. It was the last familiar landmark they were likely to see, and she was more than a little afraid to leave it behind. But their friends needed them. Laurel needed them.

"Ready?" Robbie asked.

"Ready." Stefani nodded, not feeling at all prepared. They headed into the gloomy forest.

CRISO
SORA

CHAPTER SEVEN

They'd been walking for at least an hour when the animal track they were following spilled them out into a small clearing.

Stefani gazed around at the open space and the crooked trees that edged up to it. "Does any of this look familiar to you?"

"Not really," Robbie said. "Maybe we should take a break."

Stefani glanced up at the open sky and kept walking. "It's tempting, but we haven't really gone very far."

A loud buzzing rose and fell in the forest ahead of them.

"What's that?" Stefani asked, stopping halfway across the open space.

Robbie tilted his head and cocked an ear to try and get

a better read on the sound. "I don't know, but it's getting louder."

"Or coming closer!" Stefani exclaimed, her eyes widening at the sight of the buzzing cloud emerging from the trees.

The cloud swooped closer, becoming a huge swarm of wasps, each one the size of a small bird, and all of them with needle-sharp stingers as long as Robbie's little finger.

Stefani stared, a look of horror in her eyes.

"Look out!" Robbie pushed Stefani down and hit the dirt beside her as the swarm of angry wasps dive-bombed past, narrowly missing them.

The horde of insects banked, swerved, and turned for another pass.

Robbie gasped in surprise. "They're attacking in a group."

"What do we do?" Stefani shouted over the growing hum of attacking insects.

"Weapons!" Robbie yelled, searching the ground for something to fight the nasty bugs.

Stefani reached back and tore the ground cloth from where it was tied to her pack. Holding one edge, she leaped up and whipped it hard in the direction of the front line of wasps. The cloth unraveled, snapping open with a crack, knocking a bunch of the wasps aside and tangling a few more in the cnvas. She slapped the cloth down hard on the ground, trying to dislodge the angry wasps caught in its folds.

Robbie grabbed up a dead branch about the size of a baseball bat and started swinging, smacking wasps out of the sky left and right.

Stefani managed to shake loose the insects that had caught in the fabric and swung it up into the air overhead, sweeping another batch of wasps from the sky.

Out of the corner of his eye, Robbie saw an extra-large, extra angry wasp diving straight for Stefani as she slapped the ground cover onto the dirt. "Duck!" he hollered.

Stefani dropped down just in time and Robbie swung hard. The branch hit the wasp with a resounding crack. The rest of the deadly swarm swerved up and away.

"Are they leaving?" Stefani stared up at the wasps.

"I'm not sure," Robbie said, as the swarm drew in on itself and then spread out again. Robbie stared up into the sky, where the wasps continued to rise higher and higher.

Stefani took a step back, A few injured insects rattled and buzzed on the ground around them and Stefani raised her foot to stomp on one that skittered along the ground toward her.

"Watch out," Robbie said. "That stinger is really sharp. It could go right through your shoe." Stefani backed away and Robbie slammed the branch down on the wriggling insect, squashing it in a spray of yellow and green. Overhead, the frenzied buzzing grew louder. The rest of the wasps had created a tight wall. Row upon row of fist-sized insects rose together as one, like soldiers marching in formation. "I think they're regrouping."

"There are too many of them," Stefani said. "And if those stingers have venom in them—"

"Even if they don't," Robbie said. "Those stingers are so big, with that many of them, they'll tear us up in no time."

"You're right," she said. "And wasps don't drop their stingers like bees do. They keep them intact and can sting over and over with them."

"Great." Robbie clutched his branch and brought it up to his shoulder. "Well, we can't outrun them, so there's really no choice except to—"

"Fight," said a familiar voice in his ear.

Robbie spun around to see who had spoken.

"Lieutenant Katar!" Stefani shouted with joy.

The Lightwing soldier hovering in the air beside them grinned and saluted. "At your service," he told them, with a sweeping aerial bow. "But it's Commander now. I've been promoted a few times since last we met." He straightened and seemed to grow taller than his normal six-inch height, his bronze and silver polished breastplate glinting in the sun.

"Much has changed in Anoria since we ventured together in search of the Nelig Stones." The fairy soldier shook his head. "And none for the better." He drew his sword and raised his eyes toward the swarm of insects overhead.

In the sky above them, the wasps had stopped climbing. They hovered in the air for a moment before turning and, row upon row, began a steep dive.

"Here they come!" Stefani shouted.

"Can you keep those nasty stingers distracted for just a few more minutes?" the Lightwing asked.

Robbie readied his club. "It's not like we were planning to go anywhere, right Stef?"

"Um, right." She flashed him a wide-eyed look, gripping the corner of the tarp in her fist.

"Excellent." The Lightwing saluted them, then sped away.

Stefani planted her feet. "I hope he has a plan."

"So do I," Robbie said, raising the branch and gritting his teeth in preparation for the oncoming assault. "So do I."

CHAPTER EIGHT

The buzzing of the wasps rose in pitch as the ugly swarm dove down on them. Robbie held the end of his makeshift bat, tightening and loosening his grip as he prepared to do battle.

"I don't know how many swings I can get with this thing before they're on us." Stefani had pulled the ground covering behind her, her arm outstretched, ready to fling it high overhead and capture as many wasps as possible.

"Just keep them off yourself," Robbie said, worry creeping into his voice.

They stood back-to-back as the first wave attacked.

Swinging with all her might, Stefani twirled the fabric in circles and figure eights over their heads, while Robbie's bat cracked, striking down the insects that managed to get through.

"Ow!" Stefani yelped as a huge wasp streaked in under their defense and scraped its sharp stinger across her cheek. As it swerved away from her, Robbie smacked it with his branch, slamming it into two other wasps that had flown in close.

"Take that!" he yelled.

Blood ran down Stefani's stinging cheek, but she ignored the pain and slapped another group of insects down with the fabric. "My arms are getting tired," Stefani shouted. "What happened to Katar?"

"I don't know, but keep fighting," Robbie urged. "I think there are fewer of them, now."

"Oh, no," Stefani gasped.

"What's wrong?" Robbie swung, connecting with one wasp and slamming into another on the backswing.

"Above the trees. There's another swarm!"

A dark swirling mass was coming at them fast. A high-pitched sound came from the cloud.

"I'm sorry," Stefani said, preparing to swing her weapon at the new threat. "If it hadn't been for me—"

The noise grew louder as the second swarm closed in, growing into the sound of separate voices raised in a battle cry.

Stefani swung back the cloth, but instead of swinging it forward, she let out a whoop.

"Stef, are you okay?" Robbie swatted at a pair of wasps that had suddenly zipped down from above and swerved away from him at the last moment. "What—"

"Robbie, it's the Lightwings!" Stefani cheered as the Lightwing soldiers, with their old friend Katar in the lead, charged at the swarming insects in a tight battle formation, splitting off at the last moment to engage the wasps in aerial combat.

Robbie and Stefani swung at their remaining assailants with renewed energy, making sure to avoid hitting any of the Lightwing troops.

The wasps were larger than the Lightwings, their ugly stingers reaching further than the outstretched swords of their opponents. But the fairy soldiers were battle-trained and wore thick-looking armor made from metal and leather. Their bronze-covered helmets shone in the sunlight and they wielded shields made from reinforced nutshells. They darted in and around one another, clashing with the wasps in deadly melees, sword against stinger. Attacker became defender and the battle turned. One by one, dead and wounded wasps rained down onto the ground where Stefani and Robbie, who no longer had to worry about the terror from above, put the injured ones out of their misery.

Once the last of the wasps were finally dead or chased away, Katar flew down to rejoin Stefani and Robbie. His armor, now splattered with insect gore, was no longer shiny. And his face was red with effort.

"Katar, that was spectacular," Stefani said, panting.

"You are injured," Katar said.

Stefani reached up to touch her face. Her fingertips came away covered in half-dried blood. "It's just a scratch."

"Perhaps," said Katar, "but it should be tended to. And it should be watched to be certain none of the insect's poison was left behind."

Stefani cringed. She had forgotten about the possibility of venom. Since it hadn't actually stung her, it was unlikely, but the creatures in Anoria were different from home. She'd have to clean the wound really well. "I have a first-aid kit in my pack, but first may I offer you a place to rest?" She stood up straight and tapped her shoulder lightly with her fingertips.

Katar surveyed his troops, searching the clearing with a grim look. "Thank you for your kind offer, but I must see to my own wounded first."

Stefani viewed the area with fresh eyes, seeing it as Katar must. The Lightwings had taken fewer casualties than the wasps, but there were still a number of injured soldiers. Several of them lay on the ground, their comrades huddled around them. Either they were unable to fly or... She sucked in a breath, afraid she would lose control if she let her emotions loose. She looked away, trying not to think about the fairy soldiers who had died protecting them.

She sighed as she dug into her pack for the first-aid kit. "Here." She opened the kit and laid out the bandages and ointments. "The least we can do is offer what we have to help."

The Commander sniffed at the ointment. He tested the weight and thickness of the bandages, then shook his head. "Our own medicines will need to do. These are unfamiliar to me and the heavy material you use would be too thick and weighty for Lightwings. But I thank you for your offer." He gave her a quick salute before flying away.

Stefani took out a gauze pad, poured some water on it and used it to wipe away the dried blood on her face. She let out a hiss as the wet gauze scraped against her wounded cheek.

"Here, let me help you with that." Robbie held out his hand for the kit.

By the time Robbie had finished cleaning and bandaging her cheek, the Lightwing officers had already begun to set watches. Katar flew across the open space, organizing the rest of the soldiers into small units, sending some to rest and others to help with the wounded. Once the soldiers had their orders, Katar flew back to where Robbie and Stefani stood. "We are grateful for your help," he told them, lighting on Stefani's shoulder. His gaze swept downward. Around their feet, lay dozens of dead wasps.

"We're the ones who are grateful," said Robbie, looking down at the mess. He took out his water bottle and took a swig. Stefani took out her own water bottle, then glanced at Katar, who sat on her shoulder busily cleaning his sword. "May I offer you some water?"

"I could use a drink, but water will do for now." He smiled and winked, then gave his sword a final swipe before slipping it into his scabbard.

"We're lucky you came along when you did," Robbie said.

"Not so much luck," Katar said after he had drunk his fill of water from the bottle cap Stefani had filled for him. "We were tracking the mad swarm."

"Mad swarm?" Stefani screwed the lid back onto the bottle.

"Indeed. The wasps are usually not so dangerous, but as of late they have attacked our people unprovoked. We lost more than a dozen harvesters in the last strike." His face drew tight with anger. "It's one thing to lose soldiers," he told them, his voice harsh, "but to lose innocents, those untrained for battle, gatherers who had simply gone out to search for much needed seed and nectar..." He hung his head. "Had we known the swarm had grown so dangerous, we would have sent more soldiers to guard them, but..." His words trailed off.

"I'm sorry," Stefani said. "That's awful."

Katar nodded. "Once alerted to what had happened, we gathered the company and set out after them. I had just set the main guard to rest and sent out scouts, when something drew me here."

"It's a good thing. I don't like to think what would have happened if you hadn't found us," Robbie said.

"Happenstance led us to meet up with you, but tragedy, not luck, brought us this way. However, I am still glad to see you both."

"It's good to see you, too." Stefani gave him a small smile. "I just wish it was under better circumstances."

Robbie pushed at a dead wasp with the toe of his boot. "What made them so angry?"

"And are they always so big?" Stefani stared at the fist-sized insect.

36

Katar shrugged. "They are no larger, nor smaller than usual. And they have ever been an aggressive species, but what's driven them mad is the sickness. That, combined with the lack of resources because of it." He shook his head. "Though, it appears these have stingers longer than the norm."

He flew down from where he perched on Stefani's shoulder and landed beside the nearest wasp's body. He drew his sword and slashed downward, cutting the long stinger from the wasp with a loud crack. He gripped the stinger like a weapon. "The Queen will need to be informed of this, and I want to be sure she knows there is no exaggeration in our reports." He tucked the stinger into his belt, before flying back up to eye level. "While I am happy to see you again, I am curious what has brought you back to Anoria," Katar said.

"Laurel." Stefani shivered as she said the Treemage's name.

"Laurel? She is well then? We heard she was taken by the disease." Katar's tone changed to hopefulness. "The Queen will want to know of your return and that the King's Mage is well." He glanced around. "But if she brought you here, where is she now?"

"We don't know." Stefani bit her lip.

Robbie frowned. "She didn't exactly *bring* us here. More like she called to us. To Stefani, actually."

"She spoke to me in a dream," Stefani said. "She called to me, asking for help."

"Then the news of her illness may after all be true?" Katar gave them a worried look. "But how then was she able to work her magic to penetrate beyond the Gate of Worlds?"

"I don't know. I kept having this dream where she was calling my name, telling me she needed us, that Anoria needed us. And she mentioned the Queen. But I think it was actually the ring that brought us here." Stefani touched her fingertips to the silver band.

"If the Queen is your goal, then it is a lucky thing we found you here. For that is our intended direction." Katar eyed the ring. "But I would take great care with that. It must be a very powerful talisman to open the Gate of Worlds."

"I agree." Robbie frowned down at the bodies of the giant wasps that littered the ground. "And it almost turned out to be a one-way ticket from the start."

CHAPTER NINE

Robbie and Stefani sat in what little shade the dry, brittle-branched trees had to offer, as Katar and his officers readied the troops to move.

"Are you okay?" Robbie asked.

"Not really," Stefani said, watching the Lightwings wrap their wounded soldiers in the hammock-like netting that would be used to fly them home.

Robbie would have offered to help carry the injured fairies, but there were too many of them. It made him angry to think of the ones who had not survived. His gaze travelled over to the spot where seven small mounds of dirt now broke the otherwise even ground.

The wasps had been piled in the center of the clearing and burned in an attempt to keep the disease from spreading.

"This wretched illness travels the earth, spreading to everything, no matter what we do to try and prevent it," Katar told them, frowning at the sickly trees surrounding the open space.

"Is it this bad everywhere?" Robbie asked.

"It is for Lightwings and Glimmering. And from all reports, it's no better for any other creatures." He glanced at the smoldering ash heap in the middle of the clearing.

Once the bodies had burned to ash, Robbie had used most of a water bottle to help douse the fire. The bitter scent of charred insects clung to the clearing as Lightwing soldiers sifted the ashes to be sure no embers remained. It wouldn't take much to set the whole forest aflame in its current condition.

"It's so horrible," Stefani said.

"Yeah." Robbie picked up a small stone and rubbed the dirt from it. "It's not much like it was here the first time, is it? The whole place has changed. And not in a good way."

"You're right, but things have changed even more than I expected. I mean, I knew that time passed faster here, but this other stuff . . . I never thought how bad things must be if Laurel thought she needed help from *us*." Stefani turned the ring on her finger. Its shiny surface looked dull in the shadow cast by the thin branches overhead. "I should have realized."

"How could you? And so what if you had?" Robbie said, his voice harsh. "Are you saying that if you had known how bad things were, that would have stopped you from coming?" He tossed away the rock he'd been messing with.

Stefani thought about it for a moment. "No. I would have come anyway."

"Exactly. We had to come." He gave her a meaningful look. "Both of us."

"I know." She scuffed her feet in the dirt. "But now that we're here, I have no idea what we're supposed to do. What can a couple of kids possibly do to fix any of this?"

She waved her arm at the forest and the clearing, and the Lightwing soldiers readying to return home.

"Laurel wouldn't have asked for our help if she didn't think there was something we could do," Robbie said with certainty. "We just have to figure out what it is."

A Lightwing officer flew over to where they sat. "Commander Katar asks that you prepare to travel," he said.

"We're ready." Robbie stood up and offered a hand to Stefani.

She reached out, then jerked her hand back in sudden fear.

Robbie frowned at her. "What's wrong?"

"I think we should be careful," she said, pushing herself up. "We don't really understand how this ring works. What if it really is a powerful object, but it just needs to charge up in between uses, like a battery or something."

"You mean like a capacitor," he corrected her, dropping his hand down to his side. "Good point, I guess." His lips turned down in an unhappy frown.

The Lightwing officer hovered nearby. He tried to look disinterested, but curiosity showed in his eyes.

"The ring," Stefani explained. "I think it gets activated when we, uh, touch."

"But not always," Robbie put in.

"So, it's a trust ring?" The soldier nodded at the ring on Stephanie's hand.

"A trust ring?" Stefani asked. "What is that?"

"A token given to one's true love. A promise of trust and loyalty."

"Oh, no," Robbie said. "It's not that kind of ring." He glanced at Stefani, then busied himself picking up his pack and slinging it onto his back. "We aren't—"

"No, we aren't." Stefani felt heat rising up her neck and looked away, hoping to hide her blushing. She dusted off her pants and hefted her own pack into place.

"My apologies. I've embarrassed you. I can see perfectly well that the two of you aren't." The Lightwing winked at them, then soared back across the clearing to rejoin his unit.

"What was that about?" Robbie asked.

"I don't know." She turned away.

Katar gave the signal and the troop formed up. Several scouts zipped ahead, as a ring of guards formed around the soldiers who carried the wounded. Each injured Lightwing was slung in a hammock that sagged between two soldiers.

"It's starting to feel a little more like our last quest with Katar, isn't it?" Robbie said.

"I suppose so," Stefani murmured. "I just hope Queen Karissa is more welcoming than she was the first time we were here."

CHAPTER TEN

They arrived at the Lightwing Glen ragged and tired.
The Lightwing fairies who came out to greet the returning
troops did so in quiet. Some came to help carry in the
wounded soldiers. Others searched the passing troops.

Mournful families left for their homes, knowing their
loved ones would not return to them this day. They wept
without sound, but their sorrow tore at Stefani as if the glen
was filled with wailing. She stared at the small waterfall
where they had first met the Lightwing Queen, trying to
keep back the tears that sprang into her own eyes. The
fountain no longer cascaded with tinkling laughter.

Stefani shrugged off her pack and sat beside the
trickling spring, wishing that Anoria and all its creatures
could be the way they had before. She stared into the water,

recalling their last day in this land. How the creatures had cheered them, thanking them for rescuing the Nelig Stones from Ashkell and Greenback. She shuddered, remembering their capture, their time in Ashkell's dark dungeon, and the way the angry dragon had swooped down on them as they escaped from his prison. She saw again the way the world cracked open when the powerful Nelig Stones had been brought together. Watched Ashkell's mad dive into the chasm to recover the stone she had thrown into the earth's open maw. Relived the moment the chasm had slammed shut and Ashkell had been trapped.

He, along with the great Nelig Stone, had been buried deep within the land. Was that what had caused the sickness?

"Stef?" Robbie whispered. "Is something wrong?"

She started out of her dark thoughts. Angry and frustrated—and feeling more than a little guilty—at the new trouble this land and its inhabitants now faced. "What could possibly be wrong?" she snapped.

Robbie's forehead wrinkled in confusion. "Sheesh, what'd I do now?"

"I'm sorry, okay?" She dipped her fingertips into the water and wiped her eyes, attempting to hide the tears that had pushed their way out. "It's just that I can't help thinking that all of these things, the dying trees, the sickness of the insects, and whatever else has gone wrong here, is our fault."

"Our fault?" Robbie frowned. "How's any of this stuff our fault?"

"It was us." Stefani wiped her fingers on her jeans. "We came here. We needed the Nelig Stones to get home. And I'm the one who threw the Great Stone into the chasm where it got locked with Ashkell."

"So?" Robbie shrugged. "Emrys, himself, said the Great Stone belonged to the land, that it was all connected to him. That's how he sent us... Oh. It's all connected. Soooo, you think the sickness happened because the Great Stone got locked underground?"

"What else could it be?"

"I don't know." Robbie looked thoughtful. "But then how did it bring us here in the first place, and why? I mean, didn't you find it in our world? At Hole-in-the-Rock?"

"Yes, but I'm telling you," Stefani said, "it's our fault. Actually, it's mine. I'm the one who did it. I made the choice. I'm to blame." She hung her head. Her heart felt like a stone inside her chest, but not a magical one. No, it felt like an ugly lump of slag.

"You can't blame yourself, Stef." Robbie sat down beside her and put a hand on her shoulder. "If we were only going to cause worse trouble for Anoria, shouldn't something as powerful as the Great Stone have found a way to keep us from coming here, rather than bringing us through the Gate of Worlds?" He shook his head. "Besides, you only did what you had to do. Even if this sickness might be caused by the Great Stone being locked into the earth, you saved the land from Ashkell, which would have been a worse fate than this." He waved a hand at their surroundings.

"Oh, really?" She shook her head. "Look around you, Robbie. Trees are dying, Lightwings are...dying." Her voice dropped to a whisper. "Even Laurel may be... And it's all because of what we did when we were here before. What I did."

"You don't know that, Stef."

"Yes," she said, trying her best not to sniffle, "I do."

"Fine," Robbie said, exasperation in his voice. "So, what are *we* going to do about it?"

She gave him a questioning look.

"We're back in Anoria because Laurel wanted us here, right?"

"I suppose so." She picked up a stick and dragged it through the dirt at their feet, making a series of spiraling circles.

"Then we need to fix whatever is wrong. Whether or not we caused it. Which, by the way, I don't think we did. But if we did, we did it together. If there's blame to be placed, it's on both of us. So, like I said before, what are *we* going to do about it?"

Stefani sat silent, not knowing how to respond. Robbie could say it all he wanted, but none of this was his fault. She was the one who had found the Great Stone and carried it back into Anoria. She had put it within reach of Ashkell, even if she hadn't known what she carried. No. Robbie wasn't to blame for any of it, but a part of her was grateful that he was willing to carry some of the burden with her. She looked down at the circle she had marked into the dirt, then gazed at the ring on her finger, recalling what the Lightwing soldier had said. *Loyalty and trust.*

Once Katar had seen that the injured were tended to, he dismissed the rest of the troops, watching as they disbursed. Then, he flew over to where Stefani and Robbie waited.

"Queen Karissa will likely send for you soon. I'm certain she will wish to see you right away." His face looked haggard and his eyes held a deep sorrow.

"Katar," Stefani said. "Are you all right?"

The Lightwing Commander looked away, then seemed to compose himself before turning back to them. "My brother's eldest was among the soldiers who were injured today."

"I'm sorry," Stefani said. "Is there anything we can do to help?"

"His condition is not dire, but the news of his injury will still be difficult on his family." He settled on the edge of the waterfall. "If not for me, he would not have become a soldier. My brother has never been happy with his choice. I fear this will strain things between us more than they already are. Yet, today he proved as brave as any Lightwing I have ever seen in battle." His eyes lit with pride as he spoke.

They sat quietly together for a moment.

The silence was broken by a blur of wings. A young Lightwing soldier zoomed over to them. She landed before Katar and placed her fist upon her heart. "Commander," she said, a bit breathless. "Queen Karissa requires your presence, along with that of your companions."

"How fares the Queen?" Katar asked.

The messenger eyed Stefani and Robbie before continuing. "She is the same as when you left."

Katar sighed. "Let the advisors know we have received the Queen's summons. Tell them we will come to the royal bower shortly."

"Commander? Will you be quartering with the men tonight, or should I tell Moth—"

"You are dismissed," Katar said with a wave of his hand.

"Yes, sir." The Lightwing said, frustration in her voice. In the blink of an eye, she was gone.

Katar looked after her. "My daughter," he said with a shrug. "She is having a difficult time understanding how to separate duty from family."

Stefani and Robbie exchanged looks, but said nothing. They both knew how difficult family could be.

"I didn't know you were married, much less that you had a daughter," Robbie said.

"Two," Katar said. "I have two daughters and three sons. They are the lights of my life." He glanced off in the direction his daughter had gone. "I am proud of each of them, but I worry what will become of them if this sickness continues." He paused a moment, then continued in a low voice. "There is something you should know." He glanced around them before continuing. "The Queen is fading. She is not what she once was."

Stefani was suddenly afraid. As much as she and Queen Karissa had not seen eye to eye, she didn't wish anything bad on the small queen. "She isn't dying, is she?"

47

"No," Katar said with a frown. "This is something much worse. Something that has not happened in many generations."

Stefani's throat grew unexpectedly tight at the news of the Queen's illness. "What could be worse than dying?" she asked.

"As I told you. The Lightwing Queen is fading."

CHAPTER ELEVEN

"Fading?" Stefani said, as they traversed the glen, leaving the sad little waterfall to run its course alone. "I don't understand."

Katar stood on Robbie's shoulder, guiding them.

They followed a narrow path to a place that had once been leafy and green. The trees here were less dry and brittle than most of the forest they had seen so far, but even here the sickness showed. Dead leaves littered the ground, while dried moss clung to the rocks. Withered stalks stuck up in tufts like unruly witch's hair.

"Our people are long-lived," Katar told them from his perch. "But the typical lifeline of our Royals has ever been even greater in comparison. Many live hundreds of turns before passing back to the earthen realm."

Robbie pushed aside stray brambles as they passed, letting them go once Stefani had her hand on them, so they wouldn't snap back and slap her.

"So, they live and...pass away, like anybody else? Just after a lot longer time?" Robbie asked in a quiet voice.

"Normally, yes," Katar replied.

"Normally?" Stefani let go the branch she was holding aside and it whipped back behind her.

"Once in a while," Katar spoke slowly, choosing his words with care, "a Lightwing will simply fade, growing fainter over time. It's a cruel fate. Not a passing back to the realm as is a proper ending, but a fading away from all we know and love."

"I bet it's hard for the families, too," Robbie said, emotion making his voice thick. He focused on the path ahead.

They walked the rest of the way in silence, arriving at a place that would have been lush before the plants and trees had begun dying. What had once been thick overgrowth, was now a tangle of thin creepers. Almost no green remained upon the stringy vines that arched overhead. It looked like a haunted woodland, not the home of a fairy queen. A light breeze had picked up. The branches above them shuddered and shifted in the wind.

Atop a huge tree stump covered in yellowed moss, stood a feather-lined nest the size of a car tire. And in the middle of the nest, upon a bed of silk and wool, rested the Lightwing Queen. She leaned against a pile of pillows, a silken coverlet over her lap. Her face was pale. Her waiting attendants sat on the edge of the nest, watchful. They seemed tense, as if expecting something bad to happen at any moment.

"Wait here," Katar said, stopping a few feet away from the queen's resting place. He flew forward, landing to kneel upon the edge of the nest. "Greetings, Queen Karissa." He bowed his head and waited for the queen to answer.

"Oh, get up, Katar." Queen Karissa waved a blurry hand at her commander. "And you two, step forward." She sat up as she spoke.

Katar stood and Robbie and Stefani moved closer to the queen. Up close, she looked like a picture out of focus. Even the queen's clothing was soft edged, blending in with the fabrics around her. Robbie's caught himself squinting to try and see the queen more clearly.

"My goodness. You look...exactly the same." Queen Karissa shook her head. "How long has it been since last we met?"

"In our world, it's been about six months," Robbie said. "But here—"

"Truly? Only six moons?" Queen Karissa seemed more surprised than Katar had been at their unchanged appearance. "Katar, how long? How many seasons since we were last visited by our enchanting guests?" She gave them a quirk of a smile.

"Many tens of turns, my queen." Katar held out his hands. "Too many for a soldier to count."

"Stop being evasive," Karissa scolded him. "I have not forgotten how old I am." She pursed her lips. "No matter. At least, I shall not grow withered and wrinkled before I pass." She held up a hand before her face and frowned at it.

Katar opened his mouth to respond, but she cut him off before he could say anything. "Now, tell me why you are here with us, this time." She waved at Robbie and Stefani. "The last time you visited our land was quite . . . eventful."

"To be honest, we're not sure." Stefani shrugged. "Laurel called to me. At least I think she did." She paused, a look of worry on her face. "I don't really know for certain. I was asleep, but it didn't feel like a dream."

"So, you're not wanting to go home as before?"

"No. I mean, yes." Stefani played with the ring on her finger. Robbie recalled how much she hadn't wanted to return home when they had started out on their first journey through Anoria, and how that had changed. How she had discovered the importance of home and family during their travels.

"Yes," Stefani finally said. "But not yet."

"We think there's something Laurel needs from us first," Robbie added. "We think we're here for a reason. There's something we're supposed to do."

Stefani gave him a grateful look.

The little Queen's ghostly eyes seemed to widen in surprise, but Robbie couldn't be sure. It might only have been the flickering shadows cast from the shivering branches overhead.

"Commander Katar," Karissa said, her voice suddenly harsh. "We must shore up the borders."

Katar glanced back at Stefani and Robbie, then turned to the queen and gave a slight bow. "I am ever at your service, my Queen. But our troops are already spread thin—"

"I don't want excuses!" The queen sat up. Her pale wings fluttered rapidly, barely raising her up a few inches before she dropped back onto her bed in exhaustion. "If there is some doom approaching, we need to be prepared. We must protect the Lightwings at all costs." She coughed and panted and her attendants resettled her, draping a light coverlet over her that appeared to float above the queen's lap, rather than lying on her.

"Please, do not overtax yourself," Katar said. "You know it only—"

"I know what it does." Queen Karissa waved her attendants away. They floated back a bit, but hovered nearby. "And you know that I have no one to entrust the crown to. No heirs remaining in my line. The continued existence of the Lightwings must be assured before I... before I am no longer able to protect them. My magic grows as thin as I do." She held up her hand before her face, once more, then let it drop into her lap. "I want our borders closed. It is the only way to protect our people once I am gone."

"But what of the envoy?" Katar held out his hands to

the queen. "What do we tell the Glimmering, who have ever been our nearest allies? Shall we deny them passage across our territory and condemn their people to starvation?"

"And what about us?" Stefani asked.

"The Glimmering must help themselves. And you will need to leave our realm as soon as possible." The Queen glared at them. "Always you bring trouble to our land. And the Lightwings have trouble enough as it is."

"It's not like we chose to come here." Stefani squared her shoulders and faced off with the formidable little Queen, whose attitude seemed to bounce from one extreme to the other as they stood talking.

Robbie nudged Stefani with his elbow.

"At least not the last time," Stefani blurted. "And this time we came to help."

"Help?" Karissa let out a harsh laugh. "Help Anoria? The way you helped us the last time? In as much as you are able to see through me, I can see through you, as well. You know that our land is dying because of you. I can see it in your heart." The queen's words were filled with anger and darkness. "My people are dying because of you!"

"But," Stefani exclaimed, her shoulders slumping. "We only—"

"I am tired," Queen Karissa muttered. "Leave me."

Her attendants fluttered up and moved to usher them all from the bower.

Katar stood stiff and resolute. "You cannot sweep this away, my Queen."

She sighed and closed her eyes, as if falling into a deep slumber.

One of the attendants hovered close to Katar. "You must leave." She touched his shoulder lightly with her fingertips.

Katar refused to look at her, but he did not shake off her hand. "You know this is wrong." He placed his hand over her fingers and gave them a quick squeeze before dropping his arm and standing at attention.

The attendant shook her head. "It is a strange turn of events. She seems fine one moment, then turns somber or angry the next. And as she has become more transparent, she has become harder edged. It's almost as if she were attempting to make up for her lack of physical substance by becoming as stone."

The pair continued to whisper just loud enough for Robbie to hear. "Our numbers are already too thin to protect our borders and we have too many foes. Now, she would have us increase that number by making our allies into enemies. It makes no sense."

"I think to her, it does." The attendant fairy took her hand from Katar's shoulder. "I will see you later at home?"

Queen Karissa's angry voice broke into their conversation. "Even my royal attendants no longer know their places. Must I call in the guard to get respite in my own chambers?"

"Go." The attendant swooped back to the queen's side and began fussing with the pillows and coverlets, speaking in low tones. The way she treated the queen, she might have been putting a small child to bed.

When Robbie and Stefani had first arrived in Anoria, the queen had been stern, but she had at least treated them fairly. This shadow queen, however, was no longer the wise woman they had encountered on their last trip. Queen Karissa had lost more than her physical presence.

Katar rose into the air. "We must leave...for now." He flew past them, his eyes hard, and his face pinched in anger and frustration.

CRSO
SOCR

CHAPTER TWELVE

They followed Katar out of the Queen's royal chamber
and back through the woods. They had to work to keep
up with the Lightwing, who set a hard pace. He would fly
ahead, then arc back, doing a quick turn behind them.
Then he would shoot forward again. Clearly, his anger had
filled him with excess energy.

It seemed to Robbie that they followed a different path
than they had on the way in, but his mind was too full of
other questions to give it much thought. "Katar," he finally
asked, on one of the Commander's circles back, "I was
wondering if you know . . . I mean, if the Glimmerings are
starving . . . Do you know if Gamdol is all right?" After
Robbie had saved Gamdol from drowning when he'd fallen
out of the small boat during their ride though the rapids,

they'd become as close as brothers. It wasn't fair that his friend was so far away. Wasn't fair that the Glimmering were in such trouble. "Do you think he'll be okay?"

Katar slowed, then hovered. His face was red, his mouth a grim line. Finally, he stretched out a hand toward Robbie's shoulder. "May I?"

"Of course." Robbie shifted the strap of his pack to make room for the Lightwing Commander.

Katar lit on Robbie's shoulder and huffed in a few deep breaths before he spoke. "First of all, you should know that our friend, Gamdol, has long been a great elder of his people and my good friend." His voice was filled with pride. "It has been an honor for me to be one of the great quest companions. There are those who understand what a kingdom ruled by a king as selfish and self-absorbed as Ashkell would have been like. Though, as you can see, there are now some who grumble that what took place on the quest for the Nelig Stones was not heroic. Rather, they suggest that what you...what *we* did on that fateful journey, has been the cause of all our ills since."

Stefani's face fell. "I know that part of it was us just trying to get home. But after everything that happened, I thought we'd actually helped."

"Yeah," Robbie said. "Emrys even threw us that big party."

"Indeed." Katar gave them a nod of respect. "And, as I said, there are those who know the truth of your hearts and the valor of the quest. But there are some who feel the need to have someone to blame for their ills. And, in this case, they have *us*."

"So, Gamdol is really old, now?" Robbie asked. His throat felt tight and his head ached.

"Not by Lightwing standards, I suppose, but to you, and to the Glimmering, he is quite . . . aged." Katar had led them to a small grotto a short distance from the queen's bower. A tiny spring fed a shimmering pool that sat beneath an outcropping of rock. "Drink. The water here is clean and it will refresh you. And it appears we have much to discuss." He leaped off Robbie's shoulder and swooped down to the edge of the water in a graceful arc.

Stefani slipped off her pack and flexed her shoulders. She kneeled at the edge of the little pond and dipped cool water into her cupped hands.

"I was really hoping to see him, again." Robbie tossed his pack onto the ground and flopped down next to it.

"I understand," Katar said. "However, I am told he no longer travels. I am certain that the Glimmering emissary would be happy to deliver your greetings to our old friend."

Stefani sat back on her heels. "We should refill our water bottles while we're here," she said, holding a hand out toward Robbie.

"Yeah. Sure." Robbie drank the last of his warm water and handed the bottle to Stefani. "So, this emissary. What's he like?"

Katar leaned over and rinsed his hands in the pool, then splashed his face. "Not much like our old friend, Gamdol, I'm afraid. Less of a venturing spirit." He took out a small bit of cloth and dried his face and hands with it, then tucked it back inside his uniform jacket. "I will make a point to introduce you before the emissary's party leaves to return to the Glimmering lands. You could send a message to our old friend. I'm certain he would be pleased to hear from you." He shook his head. "Though, I wish I had better news to offer him."

"Wait." Stefani sat back on her heels, a half-filled water bottle in her hand. "You said the Glimmering need food. That they came here to ask permission to cross Lightwing territory in order to forage. How can you send them away without helping?" She set the bottle down on the ground with a thump. "We need to go back and talk to Queen Karissa."

"There's no use." Katar hopped down from the rocky

edge of the spring. "You saw her. You heard her." His voice was gruff with emotion.

"Yes, I did." Stefani crossed her arms. "But she isn't herself."

"Exactly," Katar told her. "There's little left of the Queen you knew."

Robbie opened his pack and rifled through it.

"But someone needs to reason with her," Stefani insisted.

"There is no reasoning." Katar growled.

"I think you're wrong." Stefani stood up. "Robbie what are you looking for?"

"Nothing." He continued to dig through his bag.

Stefani shook her head at him. "I know I wasn't open to the Queen's advice when we first met," she said, "but I finally got what she was trying to tell me. And it really helped." She wiped her hands on her jeans. "Maybe, I can return the favor." She gazed off into the bleak forest.

"Katar," she said suddenly, "we need to talk to that Glimmering emissary."

"It will do no good," Katar told her.

"We won't know that until we try. Robbie?" She glanced over at him.

He continued to search through his things.

"Okay, then." Stefani nodded to Katar. "I guess it's up to us."

***

Stefani stood in the shadowy corner of a small copse of withered trees. Dried weeds clutched at the base of the trees, as if clinging to life.

She shivered and pulled her hoodie shut, zipping it with fingers that shook more from nerves than cold. A noise startled her into nearly shrieking before she recognized the sound of Katar's wings humming softly as he lit upon her shoulder.

"You scared the life out of me," she hissed, keeping her voice low.

"My apologies." He gave her a small shrug. "But calling out to warn you I was coming seemed inappropriate under the circumstances."

"Is the envoy coming?"

"No," he told her. "He says he will not be bargained with in the shadows. He will deal only directly with the queen."

"But she told you to send him away."

"Indeed. We are stuck at a crossroads without a map."

She glanced around at the dying forest. "Now, what do we do?"

"We must find a way to convince the queen to relent without involving him."

"Why do grownups have to be so stubborn?" Stefani said in frustration.

"I could say the same thing about the young." He might have been joking, but Stefani was pretty sure he meant it.

"Maybe Robbie has an idea." Stefani doubted it. Robbie had been acting really odd. When they'd told him what they were going to do, he'd just shrugged and said, 'I doubt that'll do any good,' and kept searching through his pack, as if he'd lost something important.

When they reached the copse where they'd left Robbie, it was empty. A dozen or so tiny shimmering lanterns that had been hung among the branches cast pools of light upon the ground beneath the trees. Beyond them, darkness clung to the woods.

Robbie's pack lay on the ground, some of his stuffed spilled out around it. "What happened?" In a panic, Stefani grabbed Robbie's pack and started stuffing his things back into it.

"More to the point," Katar said, hovering overhead. "Where is Robbie, now?"

A fluttering of wings announced the arrival of another Lightwing. "Father!" a voice called out.

Katar looked up sharply.

"I'm sorry . . . Sir...Commander Katar." The young Lightwing messenger from earlier hovered before Katar, her face filled with anxious embarrassment.

"Never mind protocol," Katar said, kindly. "Stefani is a friend. Stefani, this is my daughter, Ensign Ranya Stormwind. Her mother is of the Windflights."

Stefani jumped up, still gripping Robbie's pack. "Hey, I mean, hello."

The ensign started to salute, caught herself and gave Stefani a small airborne bow instead. "Honored."

"Now," Katar broke in. "What has your wings in a flurry?"

"Queen Karissa. The boy visitor."

"Robbie?" Katar asked.

"Yes," Ranya squeaked.

"What about him?" Stefani asked dropping Robbie's pack. "Is he all right?"

"He came to see her. Uninvited." Ranya bounced excitedly in the air. "She said to send him away, but he won't go."

"Oh." Katar leaped high into the air and zipped away. Ranya's wings flashed as she followed him, still going on about Robbie and the Queen.

Stefani ran after them. "Wait!"

***

The queen's bower was in an uproar. A crowd of Lightwings gathered before the entryway, hovering and shifting in the air, attempting to get a better view of what was taking place inside.

"What's going on?" Katar asked the nearest of the crowd.

A round fairy with ruddy cheeks and curly blond hair turned to him, his small brow wrinkled in concern. "The Queen." He nodded toward the nest. "She called us here."

"You don't think..." Ranya's face was a mask of worry.

"Hush," Katar told her. "This is not how she would have…"

"Would have what?" Stefani asked, still breathing hard from her run. "Katar, what's going on?" She glanced around. "And where's Robbie?"

A sigh passed through the crowd.

Stefani stood on tiptoe to peer through the doorway into the queen's chamber. Something was happening inside.

A glittering form appeared in the opening. A Lightwing fairy covered in gold. The light from the small lanterns reflected off the golden fairy, and all the other Lightwings sank to the ground before her, their heads bowed low.

"Rise, my people," Queen Karissa's voice rang out. "I am not yet ready to leave you. And it appears I am able to come fully before you for a while longer, thanks to this young one." She gestured behind her with a shimmering hand as Robbie ducked through the doorway.

"Thank you, Robbie." The Queen gave him a graceful curtsey. "Now, bring my commanders and advisors to me. We have matters to discuss."

***

"Robbie, what did you do?"

They lay on their bedrolls beside the tiny waterfall; its narrow trickle making the barest sound. It lulled Stefani, causing her eyes to droop. It had been a long day, but she couldn't bear to sleep without knowing what had caused the queen's change of heart.

"Gold dust." Robbie yawned and stretched his arms up overhead.

"Gold dust?" Stefani murmured drowsily.

"It's light, but heavy. And the powdery bits stick to your fingers. I only had a tiny bit. Just enough to cover a Lightwing fairy. My grandfather gave it to me a long time ago."

Stefani came more awake at that. "Your grandfather?"

"Yeah."

"You never talk about him."

"Nope. And I'm not going to start now." Robbie balled up his jacket to use as a pillow and shoved it under his head. "Anyway, I just couldn't stand the whole thing. Queen Karissa fading away like that, slowly disappearing right in front of everyone." He sat up and punched his jacket a couple of times. "So I thought, you know, that maybe the powder would stick to Queen Karissa, might help stop it. Or at least make it less..."

"Less awful?" Stefani said.

"Yeah," Robbie said. "It worked. Sort of. It gave her at least enough form she felt like she could be seen again."

"So, she didn't feel invisible anymore," Stefani said. "She felt like she had her power back."

"Exactly. Not that it'll probably change things much."

"Why not? Seems to me, we came to help the Queen and we did. Now, all we have to do is find Laurel, right?"

"I don't know. Is anything ever really that easy?" Robbie's last words came out a mumble as they both drifted off to sleep.

CHAPTER THIRTEEN

When they woke the next morning, there was a stir in the air. Lightwings buzzed around and overhead, busily flying here and there as if they were all on important errands.

"I'm starving," Robbie said, as they rolled up their bedding and repacked their gear.

"Me, too." Stefani combed out her hair, pulled it into a neat ponytail, and slipped a hair tie over it. "We've still got some granola bars." She held one out to Robbie.

"What, no breakfast burrito?" He took the granola bar from her.

She shook her head. "Ugh, don't even say that."

"What?" Robbie unwrapped his breakfast and took a big bite.

"You know I'm trying to go vegan." She fished around for

another granola bar for herself and sat back on her heels.

"I couldn't live on vegetables and granola bars."

"You're managing it now." She waved her still-wrapped breakfast at him.

"Not by choice."

Katar arrived as they finished their meal.

They folded up their wrappers and Stefani stuffed them in a side pocket on her pack.

The Lightwing Commander swooped in the air before them. "Thank you, Robbie, for the boon you provided our Queen. And our people."

Robbie wiped his hands on his pants. "I wasn't sure it would work."

"But it did." Katar glanced in the direction of the queen's nest, then turned back to Robbie. "We owe you a tremendous debt."

Robbie shook his head. "You don't owe me anything. You saved my life, both our lives, the last time we were here. More than once. And now again with those wasps. We can never repay that." He looked down at his shoes for a moment, then raised his eyes to Katar. "That's what friends do for one another. Right?"

"Indeed," Katar replied. "As you did for Gamdol."

"Yeah." Robbie shoved his hands into his pockets.

"You would be proud of the leader he has become."

"I was already proud to call him my friend," Robbie said. "A long time before he became an elder of the Glimmering. I just didn't realize it. Or that he would grow old so fast."

Katar cleared his throat. "I have actually come to ask if you will join the Queen in greeting the visiting Glimmering emissary. Both of you." He nodded toward Stefani, who had been sitting quietly, listening to their conversation.

"Me, too?" she asked. "But the gold dust was all Robbie's idea."

Katar nodded. "Queen Karissa wishes you both to attend this meeting."

Stefani looked at Robbie. He shrugged and leaned his pack against the closest tree.

When they arrived at the Queen's nest, there was no longer a huge crowd. Only the usual attendants and guards. They hovered, sat or stood on nearby branches, talking in low voices that quieted when Stefani and Robbie stepped into the clearing. The Lightwings faced them, bowing and curtsying as they approached.

Robbie felt his cheeks warm. Stefani's neck flushed in embarrassment. Katar continued forward, acting as if this happened every day. He led them into the grove of trees with the overhead branches that served as an arched roof.

Robbie was surprised at the change in the interior of the queen's palace room. Queen Karissa sat upon a throne carved from living wood that normally would bud and bloom. Now, the tiny leaves on it were pale and wilted. But the queen sat upright, the picture of her old regal self. In the light that filtered through the trees, the glittering gold that dusted the Queen from head to foot shimmered.

Karissa waved them closer.

"Thank you." She nodded at Robbie. "You have done a great service for me. And our people." She waved a hand at the room, but it was clear she meant the gesture to take in all the Lightwing subjects within the realm. "No matter the hardships that have come to us, you continue to serve the land of Anoria. For that we are grateful." She squared her shoulders and clutched her hands together, then held her head high. "We have little to spare these days, but what we have is yours for the asking. What boon would you have for your service?"

Robbie glanced at Stefani, then back at the tiny queen. "Thank you, Queen Karissa," he said. "We don't want a reward. Only...if you or your people could help us find Laurel Silverbark, we would really appreciate it."

Queen Karissa stared at him a moment in thought. "If anyone knows where the Treemage can be found, it is

Aurien."

Robbie nodded. "We kind of figured he might know. But we could use help getting to his glen."

A frown darkened the queen's face. "As you have seen, our people face danger from all sides. We cannot spare a full escort," she said. "However, we will provide you with a guide who can show you the way. Commander Katar, please see to it."

"Yes, your majesty." Katar bowed to the queen. "With your leave, I will send Ensign Ranya Stormwind."

The queen's eyes widened as if in surprise, but she nodded once, granting her permission.

Stefani wondered if a single fairy soldier would be enough, especially one as young as Katar's daughter seemed to be. Their last journey across Anoria had required three, not to mention Gamdol and Laurel—but she didn't say anything. It was clear, the Lightwings—and everyone else in Anoria—were doing the best with what they had. And Katar must trust his daughter's abilities to send her off on such a mission. Stefani only hoped the journey would be uneventful and that Ranya would return safely to her family afterward.

Queen Karissa turned back to face the crowd. "As to the matter of the Glimmering, we must close our borders."

There was a buzzing from the onlookers. The Glimmering envoy's face folded into an angry frown. His pale green hands gripped his cycle stick so tightly, his knuckles showed white. He was taller than Gamdol had been, and older. Katar was right about this Glimmering not being the venturing type. His cycle stick had almost no carving on it.

Stefani started forward, but Robbie touched her arm and pointed to the throne.

Queen Karissa held up her hands for quiet. "As I said, our borders will be closed." She raised her voice to be heard above the noise. "However, we understand that our neighbors are in need."

The envoy tilted his head expectantly, hands relaxing on his cycle stick.

Queen Karissa struggled to gather energy, as if speaking was a great ordeal. Robbie recalled Karissa's past confidence. His chest tightened. Slowly disappearing from the people you loved and those who cared about you must be horrible.

After a moment, the Lightwing Queen continued. "We will allow a small number of Glimmering harvesters to pass through the southwest section of our domain."

"Your Majesty," the envoy said. "We are grateful for your generous...dispensation. But the Glimmering need more than passage for our harvesters. We need the opportunity for our scouts to seek out new locations for our settlements."

Queen Karrissa's jaw tightened. "It is a time of hunger and difficulty for all." She clasped her hands together, but stopped when specks of gold dust drifted off of her and settled at her feet. "But my responsibility is to the Lightwings. You may accept my offer. Or not." She leaned back, as if exhausted. "Now, please allow me some peace and privacy."

Her subjects bowed and curtsied as they backed away. The glum-looking Glimmering gritted his teeth and bowed his head at her dismissal. A young Glimmering stood beside the envoy. She stared at Robbie, her large eyes open wide, as if afraid he might disappear if she blinked. As soon as she saw Robbie looking at her, she ducked back behind the envoy. The older Glimmering turned his gaze, squinting at Robbie. Then, without another word, he spun on his heel and left the Queen's reception area.

So, much for sending a message to Gamdol, Robbie thought.

The young Glimmering glanced back at Robbie once more as she trailed after the envoy.

CRRO
ROCR

CHAPTER FOURTEEN

They left the Lightwing sanctuary early the following morning. No crowd gathered to see them off.

Katar saluted his daughter in the stiff manner of a commanding officer, and Ranya snapped a salute in response. Stefani was sure she saw the glisten of tears in the Commander's eyes as he turned and flew away in a blur.

Ranya watched as he winged out of sight. "His responsibilities to his Queen and people require that he stay close." Both pride and sadness colored her voice.

Stefani stepped carefully, guilt dragging at her more than the weight of her pack, which was heavier with the added few supplies the Lightwings had been able to provide. Both she and Robbie had tried to dissuade the Lightwings from giving them so much, but they had insisted. It was the Queen's bidding to give them as much as possible in the hope that their quest would be successful. Everyone's hopes seemed to be placed on their backs with the food and water.

Ahead of her, Ranya scouted the winding path through the dark woods. The Lightwing would fly forward in a zigzag pattern, then zip back to make sure Stefani and Robbie still followed. Robbie trailed behind Stefani. He'd been especially quiet since they'd left the Lightwing glen and seemed to keep his distance from her for some reason.

Stefani rubbed her thumb along the silver ring. The Lightwing queen was still fading. Stefani wondered where Laurel might be. Was she fading like Queen Karissa? And if the land continued to die, would Laurel be able to survive? Would any of the land's creatures? And how could she and Robbie possibly help, if Laureal and Aurien couldn't?

Ranya was ahead, just turning to fly back to them when Stefani heard Robbie step lightly up behind her. "Don't look back," he said quietly.

Stefani started to turn. "What is it?"

"I said don't," he warned. "And keep walking."

"What's going on?" Stefani asked, staring at the path ahead.

"I think we're being followed." Robbie stayed behind and to her left, keeping pace.

A shiver ran cold fingers up Stefani's spine. What could be following them? Could it be a fireworm? She recalled Longscar and his hissing fire-breathing minions and her breath caught in her chest. "What should we do?"

"I don't know," Robbie said. "I'm not even sure what we're up against." He was quiet for a moment.

"Maybe Ranya can circle back and scout out what we're dealing with," Stefani said.

"That's as good a plan as any," Robbie said. "I'll fall back, put a little distance between us, so you can tell her the plan."

Stefani nodded. She tried to remain calm and listened intently as, behind her, Robbie's footsteps grew farther away.

Ranya flew back to her and hovered at eye level to give her an update. "I've scouted the path up ahead. It's still clear for a bit, but there's a fallen tree across it a little way off. It's too big to go over. We'll have to go around."

"That might be a problem," Stefani said in a low voice.

"Why?" Ranya gave her a puzzled look.

"First, I need you to act like nothing is wrong."

"Something is wrong?" The Lightwing's wings buzzed nervously.

"We're not exactly sure," Stefani said. "But Robbie thinks someone or something might be following us."

Ranya floated higher to glance back over Stefani's shoulder and frowned. "I don't see anything."

"Robbie thought it might be a good idea if you pretended to scout ahead like normal, but instead maybe went around and checked the path behind us?"

Placing a hand to her sword hilt, Ranya nodded. "All right. But if you get to the tree before I return, you'll need to head toward the root end to get around it. The upper branches are stacked against a copse of thick trees. There's no passage in that direction. And if something is following, you don't want to be trapped against the trunk."

"Good point," Stefani said, her footsteps faltering at the thought. "Maybe we should walk a little slower?"

Ranya shook her head. "Don't change pace. It might warn whoever is back there, that we are aware. We'll lose the element of surprise." She glanced back down the trail past Robbie. "Keep moving after you get around the tree. I'll deal with whatever is behind us and return as quickly as possible."

Stefani wasn't sure how surprise might help them. They were just two kids and a tiny fairy. Ranya was a soldier and carried a sharp blade, but if they were up against fireworms or worse, a single fairy blade wouldn't be much help. "Okay, but hurry back."

Ranya saluted her and headed up the trail, wings blurring, flying faster than Stefani thought possible. Her pack felt even heavier as it bounced against her back.

ೞೞ
ೞೞ

CHAPTER FIFTEEN

Robbie examined the huge tree that blocked their path. It had been tall and broad, and its many branches stuck up and out at all angles. The top half of it covered the path. The topmost branches had broken off in jagged spikes. Great limbs stabbed against neighboring trees.

"Anything?" Stefani asked.

"No sign of Ranya, or anyone else." He began to slide his pack off his back. "I sure wouldn't want to stumble into one of those. You'd be skewered like a fish by a spear."

Stefani shook her head at him and mouthed the words, 'Not here.' She jutted her chin at the tree that blocked their path.

Robbie nodded and resettled his pack, then raised his eyebrows at Stefani.

"This way." She pointed toward the end of the tree but before they took two steps a scrabbling noise erupted in the brush ahead of them.

They stepped back and Robbie took out his pocket knife. It wasn't much of a weapon, but it was better than nothing. He snapped open the largest blade and held it out in front of him. Beside him, Stefani gripped her walking stick like a club. Robbie gave her a nod. They weren't about to be taken prisoner again. This time, they would stand their ground and fight.

The thrashing noise grew louder. Something whipped the dried grass, snapping off twigs and branches. Robbie eyed Stefani standing there with nothing but a stick in her hands. She really was one of the bravest people he knew. Her jaw was set and there was just the slightest tremor in her hands. She was scared, just like he was, but she was prepared to fight like a true warrior. He glanced down at the knife in his hand and nearly laughed at the size of it. Then he set his feet and waited. They had no idea what they were up against, but at least they would face it together.

Something yelped and the thrashing quieted. Footsteps approached. Whoever—or whatever—it was, wasn't trying to be stealthy. Robbie and Stefani stood at the ready as a young Glimmering stepped out of the undergrowth. She was young, probably younger than Gamdol had been when they'd first met him. And her green skin was a darker shade than Gamdol's had been. She had a small sack slung across her shoulder and wore an embarrassed and angry look.

Ranya followed behind her, clearly excited. She pointed her sword in the direction of the Glimmering, urging her captive forward until they were only a few feet away from Stefani and Robbie.

"It's the Glimmering who was with the Emissary," Stefani said in surprise. "What are you doing here?"

"And why are you following us?" Robbie demanded.

The Glimmering hunched down and refused to look at

either of them.

"Speak up," Ranya commanded.

The Glimmering shot the Lightwing a dirty look over her shoulder. She clamped her mouth shut and crossed her arms stubbornly.

"You can talk to us," Stefani said. "We won't hurt you."

The young Glimmering eyed Stefani and Robbie, glancing at Robbie's knife and staring at the walking stick Stefani still held like a club.

"Oh." Stefani rested one end of the stick on the ground.

"What?" Robbie said, then realized what was going on. He folded the knife shut and slid it into his front pocket. "Sorry."

"Well, I'm not sorry," Ranya said. "And I'm not about to sheath my weapon until we know what this Glimmering is about." She hovered in the air, her sharp sword held at the ready.

The Glimmering gave the Lightwing another dirty look, then uncrossed her arms and brought up her hands.

"Look out," Ranya shouted.

Stefani raised her stick and Robbie stepped back a pace, reaching into his pocket.

The Glimmering ducked as the fairy darted in close and pointed her sword in her face. She stepped back, but made no other move, a look of frustration came over her.

"Tell us why you are following us!" Ranya demanded.

The Glimmering tilted her head to one side. Slowly, she raised one hand up, palm flat against her chest and looked at Robbie and Stefani expectantly.

"What's she doing?" Stefani asked.

"I don't know," Robbie said.

The Glimmering slowly moved her hand from her heart to her mouth and shook her head. Then she touched her ear and held her hand up.

"It looks like she's trying to tell us something." Stefani lowered her stick.

Ranya circled the Glimmering, sword still at the ready. "It might be a trick."

"What kind of trick?" Robbie said. "There are three of us and only one of her."

"And I don't see a weapon of any kind." Stefani leaned on her stick.

"I think she's trying to tell us something without talking. Maybe we should give her a chance to show us what she's trying to say," Robbie suggested.

"Maybe we should stop waving a sword in her face, too," Stefani said. "Ranya, would you mind coming over here and giving her some room?"

Ranya frowned, but did as she was asked, flying backward in order to keep her eyes on the Glimmering.

"Who are you?" Robbie asked.

The Glimmering bit her lip. Slowly, keeping an eye on Ranya, she moved her hands, pointing first to herself, then making several odd motions that made no sense to Robbie.

She repeated the gestures. Then shook her head. After a moment, she tried again. This time she used a rocking motion with her arms.

"Baby?" Stefani asked.

The Glimmering nodded, then pretended to set the baby on the ground and raised her hand slowly.

"Growing?" Robbie felt like he was playing a strange guessing game, like charades, only without any real clues.

She nodded again, then repeated the motions.

"Yes, baby that grew up," Ranya snapped. "We got that."

The Glimmering shook her head yes, then no. She held up a hand, palm out. Then she went through the baby growing motions twice in a row.

"Two babies?" Robbie asked.

"No. Wait," Stefani said. "Baby of a baby? Grandbaby?"

The Glimmering nodded excitedly and pointed to herself.

"You're the granddaughter of the Emissary?"

Another shake of her head.

Stefani gave her an odd look. "Not the granddaughter of the emissary. Then who?"

The Glimmering girl pointed to Robbie and then acted like she was shaking her own hand.

Robbie's heart dropped and spun in his chest, the realization hitting him hard. "You're Gamdol's granddaughter," he said in a whisper. What before was just a vague concept, that his friend had aged so much when he had only grown taller, became real. He shook his head. "Are you on your Second Cycle journey?

She bit her lip and looked at her feet. She shook her head *no*.

"But you were with the Emissary at the Lightwing meadow?" Stefani said. "Did he tell you to follow us?"

Another shake of her head.

"Then why?" Robbie asked, his throat still tight.

She moved her hands in a series of gestures.

"I just think she wants to come along," Stefani said. "To help us?"

The Glimmering nodded, giving Stefani a weak smile.

Ranya scowled. "Then why was she being so sneaky?"

The Glimmering motioned as if she were pushing something away, then turned as if she were leaving. She turned back to them, looking hopeful.

"She didn't want us to send her away, I guess." Stefani shrugged. "I think we should let her come along."

Robbie shrugged.

"What can it hurt?" Stefani tapped the ground with the end of her walking stick in thought.

"I don't trust her." Ranya pointed her sword in the direction of the Glimmering and glowered.

"It's not like we can't use the help," Stefani said. "We are kind of outnumbered for a journey through Anoria. Especially, with what's been happening to the land. We may not have to deal with tanglevines." She pushed at a dying plant with the walking stick. "But there are bound to be other more dangerous things along the way."

"Yeah." Robbie scanned the trees around them. "Like giant wasps."

Ranya shook her head. "We managed to catch this lurker without too much trouble."

"The more of us there are, the more we can share lookout duties," Stefani suggested.

Ranya huffed out her breath but said nothing.

Robbie looked at the Glimmering. "What's your name?"

CRISO
SOCR

CHAPTER SIXTEEN

After much gesturing and pointing, Gamdol's granddaughter was finally able to tell them her name; Sealeaf. Apparently, the time they'd spent aboard the ship during their previous adventure had made a lasting impression on Gamdol.

They traveled quickly. Ranya stood double watches to keep an eye on their travelling companion. She proved to be a good guide, though they had to make more than a few stops to allow her to scout around and regain her bearings. "The forest has changed a great deal," Ranya explained. "The landmarks are no longer as they were."

Sealeaf had nodded in agreement, but Ranya had only narrowed her eyes at the Glimmering before leading them forward once more.

As they traveled, Stefani saw exactly what Ranya meant about the drastic changes that had taken place. The trees, which had been so lush and green the last time she and Robbie passed through the forest, were now withered. Their branches drooped and leaves fell around them as if it were late fall, like back home, and not spring as it should have been here in Anoria. No birds sang, either. The forest was so quiet, it felt as if it had been dragged into a sleep, deeper than a normal winter sleep.

It's like everything is slipping into a coma, Stefani thought sourly. She wondered what it would feel like to fall asleep and never wake up. She shivered and hurried after the others.

Up ahead, the sky grew dark. Gray clouds clung to the tops of the trees. As they drew closer to that section of the forest, the air turned cold and damp. A heavy mist fell around them. The ground grew soggy and the trees turned a sickly shade of yellow. An odor of rotting things clung to everything.

Ahead, the others stopped suddenly. As Stefani approached, she heard Ranya practically shouting, "We go left."

"But Sealeaf thinks we need to go the other way," Robbie said.

"I am your guide. Sealeaf is merely a tag-along." Ranya folded her arms and glared at Sealeaf. She hovered in the air a small distance down an animal track that led off from the path they had been following.

Sealeaf stood a few feet away on another trail that led the opposite way.

Between them, Robbie stood frozen, a look of frustration on his face.

"What's going on?" Stefani asked.

Robbie shrugged. "We're having a disagreement about which way to go."

"Ranya?" Stefani said. "Are you certain that's the way

we need to go?"

"Yes," Ranya said firmly.

Sealeaf stood her ground, shaking her head. She gestured at the ground and then made a circle over her head with one hand.

Around them, moisture dripped from sagging branches. Stefani pulled her jacket out of her pack and slipped it on.

"If the Glimmering wishes to try another path, perhaps it is time to part ways." Ranya's look was severe, but her tone hinted that she was happy with the idea.

Sealeaf took a step toward Robbie and gestured for him to follow her. She waved her hand over and over, signaling for them to follow.

Robbie looked from one to the other, an unhappy frown on his face. "Do you want to leave, now?" he asked Sealeaf.

Sealeaf shook her head again, repeating the odd gestures from before.

Stefani stepped up beside Robbie. "Ranya is right. She was assigned by Queen Karissa to guide us through the forest. We need to trust her."

A tight grin spread across Ranya's face. "Thank you," she said. "Now, if you would all be so kind as to follow me." She waved up the path and started off.

Sealeaf looked at Robbie, but he only shrugged. "Stefani's right," he told the Glimmering before following Ranya.

"Come on," Stefani said. "Stay with us." She glanced at Robbie and lowered her voice. "I think he really would like you to come with us."

With slow steps, Sealeaf came toward her, but before Stefani managed to turn and head after the others, she heard a loud shout. She ran down the path that Robbie and Ranya had taken, stopping short when she ran into a tangle of sticky slime that sagged down across the path from above. A few feet in front of her, Robbie was wiping at the gooey slime that clung to his clothes and skin.

"Where's Ranya?" Stefani asked.

"This stuff is like taffy." Gloppy stuff stuck to him and strands of it clung to his hand as he tried over and over to wipe it off. He jerked his head up and pointed.

Up ahead, Ranya was stuck in a puddle of goo. Frantically, she hacked and hewed at the sticky stuff that trapped her in place. So much glop covered her wings, she could hardly move them.

All around them, more of the slimy stuff dropped from nearby trees. It dripped on the ground in thick globs. Stefani started forward, but Robbie shouted at her to stop. "Don't," he said. "I'm as stuck as Ranya." He tried to lift his foot, but the sticky slime that coated his shoe sucked his foot back down to the forest floor.

Stefani took a step back and felt a tendril of goo land on her shoulder. She jerked away, backing into a tree, but the slimy stuff came with her, sliding down her sleeve. "What is this stuff?"

"I'm not sure," Robbie said, "but it's really sticky. And it dries like rubber cement. My hand is stuck to my shirt." He tried to pull his hand away, but his shirt followed, stretching out as he moved his hand.

Stefani glanced up into the shadowy branches overhead and gasped. Above them, gliding along the tree limbs, was what looked like an army of giant slugs. Each one was longer than Stefani's arm and twice as big around. And they were headed down. "Robbie," she said, trying to keep her voice from shaking.

"Hang on. I think I can slide my foot—"

"Robbie. It's important."

"What is it?" He looked over his shoulder at her.

Stefani raised her eyes upward and Robbie followed her gaze.

His mouth fell open. "Ugh. Slugs? They can't be. They're huge!" He slid one foot across the ground and managed to move a few inches.

Ranya looked up and gasped. "No, this can't be right. The

wolf slugs don't live in this part of the forest." She struggled harder. "They live in moister climates where . . ." She gazed around at the mist-covered trees with their yellowed leaves, the mounds of springy moss, and the spongy ground. "They must have migrated here when the weather changed." She shouted, her voice edged with fear and panic. "We have to get out of here."

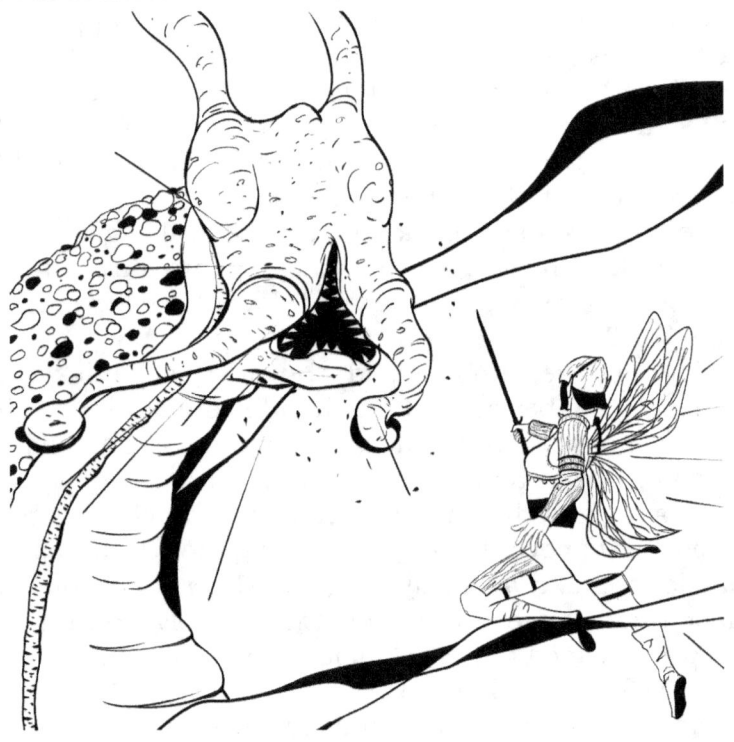

"What do we do?" Stefani said, eyeing the approaching slugs. Stefani moved away from the tree. Her left arm was stuck to her side as if it had been glued there. She jammed her walking stick into the spongy ground beside her. She tried to brush the slime off, but her right hand glommed onto her sleeve. She struggled to pull her hand away, but even her fingers seemed to be glued together. "This stuff isn't like normal slug slime."

"No," said Ranya, panting. "It's designed to trap and slow their prey."

"Prey?" Robbie asked, trying to slide his other foot forward. "Do slugs bite?"

"These do," Ranya said through gritted teeth. "Although, it won't matter to me."

"Why is that?" Robbie asked.

"I'm not big enough for them to chew."

"Oh…"

"We need to get out of here before they reach us." Ranya's voice was filled with a quiet dread. She had managed to cut through several strands of the rubbery slime, but the strain was exhausting her.

A group of slugs had reached the ground and were headed for Robbie, their thick bodies leaving a heavy trail of slime behind them.

With a plopping sound, a slug dropped from one of the lower tree branches near Ranya. Its antenna waved and twitched as it sighted its prey. It stretched its body out and began to glide toward her, mouth open to reveal rows and rows of razor-sharp teeth.

"Stay back!" Ranya yelled. She pointed her sword in the direction of the oncoming creature. The slug ignored her warning and continued forward, its yawning, spike-filled mouth a cavernous tunnel that would close around the Lightwing soldier in moments.

"I'll try and slide to you!" Robbie called out, but the slime had grown thick and hard. His progress slowed to almost nothing. Slugs came at him from every direction.

Stefani looked around desperately for some way to help her friends. Her walking stick was still stuck in the ground, but without the use of her hands, it was useless.

The slugs crept closer. Several more had slipped to the ground and were heading toward Stefani. She backed away, searching frantically for something to use against them.

Behind her, she heard an ugly thumping sound. She

spun around and froze. While she'd been watching the slugs approach her friends, a group of the ugly things had snuck up behind her. More than a dozen giant slugs oozed their way toward her, blocking the way out.

One of the huge slugs drew close. Without thinking, Stefani swung back her leg and kicked it hard. But instead of sending the slimy thing flying, her foot connected with it near the neck. And stuck. The slug opened and closed its ugly mouth, trying to turn its head enough to clamp onto her leg. "Oh!" She shook her leg, trying to stay balanced with her arms struck in place. She hopped on one foot, shaking the other foot to keep the slug from getting its mouth on her.

"Stefani. Watch out!" Robbie shouted.

She tripped over her walking stick and fell onto her back. She kicked and thrashed, attempting to get up without the use of her hands and arms, as a dozen hungry wolf slugs surrounded her. A dozen mouths yawned wide, and rows upon rows of sharp pointed teeth glistened inside.

C3ED
ED&

CHAPTER SEVENTEEN

"Hold on, Stef!" Robbie shouted as a huge slug approached his trapped foot. Its long feelers twitched and its mouth gaped wide. It was like looking into a giant pipe. A pipe with ugly rows of wicked looking teeth. "Ranya! Can you get clear?"

"No." The Lightwing stabbed at the viscous slime that glued her to the ground as the horrible slug drew closer.

After what had happened to Stefani, Robbie knew better than to try and kick the nasty thing, but his only other weapon was his pocketknife, which was practically useless. He eyed Stefani's walking stick, but it was way out of reach.

There was a sudden pop and another and another, followed by the sounds of hissing and bubbling like air flowing out of a soggy bicycle tire. Stefani struggled to sit up. All around her fat gooey slugs lay shrinking and bubbling into puddles of ooze.

The slugs in the trees surrounding the clearing stopped moving toward them. Then, the slimy beasts turned, stretching and oozing away from them, disappearing back into the trees.

"What happened?" Stefani glanced around, worried that something worse than giant slugs must be headed their way.

"They're shriveling up. It's like they've been doused with salt." Robbie shifted his feet, trying to turn in place, but the slime had thickened so much it kept pulling him back around.

"I think," Ranya said, trying to cut away the hardening slime with her sword, "Sealeaf happened." Her voice contained a mixture of relief and grudging admiration.

Stefani pushed her way onto her knees and turned to look back the way they had come. Sealeaf stood at the edge of the clearing, a long tube in one hand. In her other hand, she held some marble sized yellowish rocks.

"Are those rocks made of salt?" Robbie asked.

Sealeaf shrugged and held them out for him to see.

"Uh, I can't really see from here," he said, still struggling to turn around. "But thanks for saving us."

"Yes," Stefani said. "Thank you. And we're sorry for not listening to you when you tried to warn us. Right, everyone?"

"Absolutely," Robbie said.

Ranya had finished hacking her way out of the hardened goo and was attempting to help Robbie get his foot unstuck. She looked up from her work and made direct eye contact with the Glimmering. Then, she put her fingers to her lips and moved her hand forward and down.

A slow smile spread across Sealeaf's face.

***

"This stuff is nasty." Stefani peeled another piece of dried snail slime from her jacket sleeve. They'd limped back up the trail, and found the driest spot where they could sit and clean off the worst of the yucky stuff.

"Tell me about it." Robbie made a face. "My shoe is completely glued to my sock and my sock is completely glued to my foot." He wedged the spoon blade of his Swiss army knife inside his shoe and tried to slide it sideways to loosen the slime that had oozed inside and hardened.

Beside them, Ranya sat quietly, while Sealeaf gently peeled thin layers of the dried stuff from her back and wings. The Lightwing gritted her teeth and winced, but it was clear she was determined not to cry out.

"Doesn't that hurt?" Stefani asked, when Ranya squinted her eyes shut and grimaced.

"No more than it should." Ranya said. "And much less than being eaten by a wolf slug would have."

Robbie couldn't argue with that. He finally worked his shoe off and began scraping the hardened goo out of the inside.

"You know," Stefani said, a tiny smile quirking up the side of her mouth. "You should leave the stuff on the outside. It's probably waterproof."

"You think?" Robbie asked, eyeing his shoe.

Sealeaf looked up and shook her head.

Stefani laughed. "Not really." She held up a wiggly ribbon of dried snail slime before tossing it into the nearby brush. "If it's anything like regular snail slime, it'd probably soak up the nearest water and send you skating down the trail."

"That was naughty," Ranya told her.

"Don't you mean it was snotty?" Stefani teased.

Robbie groaned at the bad pun and flicked a wad of slime at her.

"Ugh!" Stefani dodged it and threw a chunk back, missing him and nearly hitting Ranya with it.

"Careful." Ranya told her. But Sealeaf simply flicked a

bit of the stuff back at Robbie with a grin.

Suddenly, they were tossing dried snail slime at each other and laughing uncontrollably. Ranya tried to fly up and dive bomb them with small chunks of the nasty stuff, but kept flitting sideways because the goop stuck to her left wing made her unbalanced

Soon, they all collapsed on the forest floor, panting and giggling.

"I don't know why we're all in such a good mood," Stefani said, still catching her breath from laughing so hard. "We have days to go to reach Aurien's Glen, and we're all still covered in grossness."

"I don't know about you," Robbie said, peeling off another strip of hardened slime. "I'm just happy to be alive instead of being slug food."

CRED
SDCR

CHAPTER EIGHTEEN

After another two long days of walking, they finally reached Aurien's Glen, but Stefani's great relief was short-lived. When they stepped out into the clearing, her heart filled with an ache that felt like losing a best friend. Aurien's Glen had changed even more than she had feared. The huge oak tree still stood in the middle of the field, but its leaves were pale and hung limp from its great branches. The small brook had slowed to a trickle that no longer sounded like children's laughter. Flowers no longer dotted the grassy meadow, which was now yellowed.

Aurien came to greet them, wending his way slowly across the open space of dried grass. The white unicorn had grown gaunt, his legs thin, ribs showing beneath his white coat. His horn and hooves had lost their sheen, but he still carried himself proudly.

"Greetings." He bowed formally to them, one foreleg extended, and his long, spiraled horn nearly touching the ground. "Though I am glad to see you again, I wonder what has brought you to Anoria at this difficult time?"

"I dreamed that Laurel was calling me," Stefani told him. "We came as soon as we could find a way."

Aurien bowed his head. "If Laurel has called out to you, things are more dire than we knew. She was seeking a cure for the land. We thought this would be the safest place for her to connect. But I fear this sickness goes deeper than we knew."

He led them across the meadow to the bridge that spanned the trickling stream. Stefani cried out as they drew near. She rushed across the bridge to where a familiar silhouette stood, arms stretched up to the sky. "Laurel!" She fell to her knees before the frozen form of the Treemage.

Aurien and Robbie followed her across the bridge, coming up beside her.

"What happened to her?" Robbie asked, his voice filled with emotion.

"She attempted to discover the cause of the disease that ails the land," Aurien said. "Once connected to the earth, she fell into a heavy hibernation. At first, she seemed fine, and I thought it a part of her search for answers. But the sickness quickly seeped into her limbs. Then, the essence of her slowly drained into the earth. She began sprouting branches, as you can see." He hung his head. "She has been this way since, and I have been unable to wake her."

Stefani reached out her hand and touched what would have been Laurel's ankle. Thick bark had formed over the Treemage's skin and the leaves on her head had turned a sickly yellow. "Is she . . . can she . . ."

"Physically? I believe she senses what a plant feels; the wind, the sun, the rain." Aurien gazed at Laurel for a time, before adding, "As for what she may hear, or sense beyond that, I do not know."

"How long has she been like this?"

Aurien looked up at the sky, as if calculating. "Near to two moons."

Stefani's eyes welled with tears. "Will she be all right?"

"She is losing her identity. With each passing day, she becomes less Laurel Silverbark and more...tree," Aurien told her. "If we are to save her, it must be soon."

"But how?"

"You must find the Awakener and bring him here."

"Us?" Stefani asked.

"I'm afraid there is no one else. I cannot leave the glen," Aurien said. "What magic remains, must be nurtured in order to protect what is left of my shrinking realm and its inhabitants. And Laurel."

"What about the King?" Robbie asked.

"The King, I'm afraid, has troubles of his own." He gazed up at the far-off mountain that housed the king's palace. "He will not leave Dragon Tor. Not now."

"So, who is this Awakener?" Stefani asked.

"One of the oldest beings in Anoria," Aurien said. "And, I believe, the only one left with enough magic to rouse Laurel from her unnatural sleep."

"But just us?" Robbie asked.

"As I said, there is no one else," Aurien told them. "And Laurel reached out to you. There must be a reason she called you here. Perhaps, it is to find the cure that will release her from this unnatural sleep. And you have your stout-hearted companions." He dipped his horn to indicate Ranya and Sealeaf.

"Where do we find this Awakener person?" Stefani asked.

"The Awakener does not abide in a single place, but travels the realm," Aurien said. "Normally, at this time of season, I would expect them to be in the northlands, but the way things are, they could be anywhere."

"Anoria is huge. How are we going to find someone who moves around all the time?" Robbie asked.

"By beginning your search in the most likely place," Aurien said. "The bigger problem is recognizing the Awakener when you find them."

"What does that mean?" Robbie said.

"The Awakener is changeable, much like the seasons, and can take many forms. Until one encounters the Awakener, it is impossible to know what aspect to expect."

Stefani jumped up. "If we don't know where to look, or even what they look like, how will we find them in time to save Laurel?"

"In regards to the Awakener, there will be signs that will show you the way." He grew somber. "As for being in time to save Laurel—"

Stefani slapped at the dried grass that clung to her jeans. "This is impossible." She twisted the silver ring around on her finger. "We might as well have stayed home."

Aurien was quiet for a moment. He shook back his pale mane and asked, "Do you truly wish you had never come to Anoria?"

Stefani shrugged, her eyes filled with tears.

Sealeaf stared at Stefani, mouth open in amazement, then dropped her gaze to the ground. She patted the earth with her hands.

"What is it?" Robbie asked the Glimmering.

Sealeaf gestured toward the tall oak tree, pointed to her heart, then bent her hands in front of her like they were waving at one another.

"True," Aurien said. "As long as there is still life in the land, there is hope."

Sealeaf nodded, and pointed to herself, drawing a circle around her heart. Then pointed to Stefani and Robbie.

"She believes in you, in your strength," Aurien told them. "You need to believe, as well."

"We can do this, Stef," Robbie said. "As long as we work

together."

"We had help the last time." Stefani gazed over at the still figure of the Treemage.

"You have help this time, too," Ranya said, and Sealeaf nodded.

Stefani wiped her eyes dry with her bandanna, then shoved it into her back pocket.

Sealeaf gestured at each of them, then clasped her hands together, fingers entwined.

"Yes, much stronger together." Aurien went down on one knee before Sealeaf. "It takes great heart to have hope in the face of darkness. Wisdom has come to you early in life, young Glimmering."

Clearly embarrassed by his gesture and the compliment, Sealeaf looked away. She turned back to him and touched her fingertips to her lips then moved her hand out and downward.

"Truth does not require thanks," Aurien told her, "but you are welcome."

Stefani watched them in fascination. "I wish I could understand what she says as well as you do."

"You will learn in time, as long as you have the desire to do so," Aurien told her. "You must begin by listening and watching with an open heart."

"It would be easier if you could just come with us." Robbie said. "You know, like a translator."

"You mean an interpreter," Stefani said with a tiny smile.

"What?"

"A translator translates writing from one language to another," Stefani told him. "An interpreter interprets words that people speak."

Sealeaf held up her hands.

"Or sign," Stefani added, happy to have understood at least that much.

"As I said before, I cannot leave the glen," Aurien said, breaking into their exchange. "This sickness has infected the very depths of the land. Without me, the great oak will perish and the brownies that live within it will die. And I cannot leave Laurel." He gazed at the dormant Treemage.

Stefani squared her shoulders. "Then, I guess it's up to us."

CHAPTER NINETEEN

They woke just after dawn. Aurien insisted they take
what provisions were available, but there was little to be
had. Feeling guilty, Stefani left one of their remaining
granola bars tucked in a crook of the ancient oak for the
tree sprites. Then they filled their water bottles from the
tiny rivulet.

Stefani stood before Laurel and whispered to their
friend, "Hold on, Laurel. Please."

The desperation in her voice made Robbie look away.

They hiked north. Weak sunlight struggled to reach
them through the skeletal branches of what had once been
towering pine and oaks. Dead leaves and brush covered
the ground in thick piles, hiding broken branches and deep
holes and making the way treacherous.

They ate a small meal once the sun reached its highest point, measuring out their rations and swallowing them down with a few mouthfuls of water.

"How far away are the northern lands?" Robbie asked Ranya, who sat cross-legged on his shoulder. She was supposed to be taking a break, but instead she used a small stone to sharpen her sword.

"I've never been there." She put away her sharpening stone and took out a piece of spider silk and wiped the blade till it shone. "It's well outside of Lightwing territory. And, with all the troubles, our scouts and soldiers have been busy just protecting our food gatherers. I've not been farther than Aurien's Glen before."

They were both quiet for a moment. Robbie recalled the wasps and the Lightwings who had lost their lives in the ugly battle they'd fought. Had it really only been days ago?

Ranya stood and sheathed her weapon. "I'll go forward now." She spread her wings and leaped off Robbie's shoulder, zipping ahead to relieve Sealeaf.

"It's horrible," Stefani said. "What's happening here in Anoria . . . to the land and . . . everything."

"Yeah." Robbie scratched at the back of his hand. "This place has changed so much. I mean, there were dangers here before, but now . . . It's like what isn't dead or dying is trying to destroy everything else." He gazed up at the sky. Far above and off to the west a familiar shape wriggled through the air. "Look."

Stefani followed his gaze and gasped, a worried look on her face. "What side do you think the fireworms are on?"

He shuddered at the thought of great hordes of the flying, fire-breathing creatures ruining huge swathes of land. The terrible damage they could cause, especially with the land already in such bad shape, was unthinkable. "They don't have a great track record for being good. Let's hope that if they aren't peaceful, without Greenback or Ashkell to guide them, they at least can't do anything too bad."

Sealeaf was suddenly beside them, gesturing for them to be quiet and follow her through the trees. Ranya was waiting for them at a point where the trees opened out onto a clearing. She hovered just inside the tree line and pointed. Before them stood a swathe of wrecked and burnt forest. Blackened stumps dotted the landscape, and charred branches littered the ground. A gust of wind whooshed by and picked up a swirling cloud of ash and flung it high into the sky.

The wind dropped and the ashes rained down, pattering to the earth in whispery drops. No birds sang. Nothing rustled in the nearby trees.

"This is recent damage," Ranya said, her voice low.

"How long ago?" Robbie whispered, thinking about the fireworm they'd glimpsed overhead. The heat of anger flared along his skin.

Sealeaf reached down and gathered a small amount of ash into her palm. She sniffed it, then sifted it through her fingers, letting it fall back to the ground. She held up three fingers, then four.

Ranya nodded in agreement. "A few days," she said. "No more than four."

"Fireworms." Ranya peered at the blackened area. "I see no sign of lingerers, but we need to be careful."

"We just saw one flying away."

"We'd better scout the area, then."

Sealeaf made a circling motion with her hand, then pointed to Ranya.

The Lightwing nodded again. "Stay hidden until we come back," she said.

"Hang on," Robbie said. "We're not helpless."

"No, but you are noisy," Ranya said, pointing down at their feet. "Sealeaf can tread silently, without disturbance. And I . . . ." She fluttered her wings fast enough to make a buzzing sound. "I'm only heard when I want to be."

Stefani stepped back under the trees, gesturing for

Robbie to join her. "Ranya's right. We walk like we're out hiking back in Arizona." She scrunched down to wait while their companions disappeared without a sound.

Robbie sank down beside her, trying to shut out his frustration and fear.

"Do you think it was the fireworm we saw back there that dis this?" Stefani whispered to Robbie.

"I don't know," he said, keeping his voice low. "I hope it's long gone, though. I'd really rather not have a run-in with the likes of them, again."

Stefani made a face. "Me neither. Besides," she thought of Laurel trapped in the glen, "we don't have time for this."

They were quiet for a few minutes. Robbie kept searching the clearing, nerves vibrating like they did during a close soccer match. Only, losing a game was nothing compared to being attacked by fireworms. Suddenly, Ranya swooped down beside them.

"Where's Sealeaf?" Stefani asked, her voice tight with worry.

"On the other side of the burned-out place." Ranya settled on a low branch. "There's a large burrow a short way off. Smells like a fireworm lair, but we can't tell how deep it goes. Or whether or not it's still inhabited. She's watching the entrance while we make our way around."

Ranya took out her sword and inspected the blade. "If you hear the whistle of a jarbird," she made an odd warbling sound, "it means you should run."

CHAPTER TWENTY

They tiptoed along the edge of the burned space, small puffs of ash lifting into the air with each step.

Suddenly, they heard a familiar warbling. Ranya held up a hand, signaling them to freeze. She paused a moment. The sound came again. "Run," she said, flying ahead to guide them across the remaining section of charred forest.

By the time they reached the other side, the air was filled with powdery gray ash. Sealeaf rushed up beside them, signing as she ran.

"Hurry," Ranya urged.

They sped up, all attempts at stealth forgotten. Stefani's pack slapped against her back, her lungs burning.

Behind them, arose a slithering sound. A fireworm had given chase.

They reached the end of the scorched section. Ahead, the forest loomed.

"Lead it into the trees!" Robbie shouted. "Fireworms aren't very smart. Maybe we can trick it into getting stuck."

"I heard that," a whispery voice called after them.

Stefani cringed, glancing over her shoulder to see how far back the creature was. She stumbled and almost fell when she saw the long, white scar running down the length of the fireworm that pursued them. "Oh, no."

"What is it?" Robbie yelled.

"It's Longscar."

They ran faster.

CHAPTER TWENTY-ONE

Longscar followed them on the ground as far as the tree line, then heaved upward and flapped his wings. He rose above the trees and belched a jet of fire.

The scent of smoke dripped down from above and Robbie realized their mistake. "We need to get out of here before we get cooked alive!"

But the farther they went, the closer the trees grew. Soon they were squeezing sideways to fit through the tight spaces. "We need to go back," Stefani huffed as she spoke. She stopped and leaned her back against an enormous tree trunk, trying to catch her breath.

"Yesssss, do come back, my juicy little haressssss," Longscar hissed. "I remember you," the monster called in a hoarse voice. "You're friendsss of that traitor king!"

"What's he talking about?" Ranya flitted this way and that, seeking a path of escape that the others might fit through.

"We've met him before," Stefani said, staring up at the tangle of dry leaves and brittle branches overhead.

"Yeah. He and his buddies were working for Ashkell the last time we were here." Robbie peered up, trying to see through the dense canopy of leaves.

Sealeaf's eyes went round in surprise.

"But that was ages ago." Ranya said. "And what does he mean about the traitor king?"

"I have no idea," Robbie said. "I thought the fireworms signed a new treaty with Emrys after everything that happened with Ashkell and Greenback."

"So, they did," Ranya said. "A treaty that, as far as the Lightwings know, has lasted since that time."

"It sure sounds like something has changed." Stefani cringed as another blast of fire scorched the tops of the trees overhead.

Sealeaf waved at them from a narrow opening between the trees.

Ranya buzzed over to check it out. "Over here," she said, trying to keep her voice down. "Sealeaf found a way through. I think you can fit, if you take off your packs and keep low."

They followed the Lightwing, moving as silently as possible while ducking beneath branches and helping one another climb over winding roots.

Above them, Longscar flapped his great wings, belching fire at the dying trees, but the weak flames he spit never quite caught. Instead the leaves and branches only smoked and smoldered.

The travelers kept going, crawling on their bellies for long stretches. After what seemed like forever, the sound of the fireworm faded. The only noise was the rustle of branches they brushed against and the sound of twigs and leaves that shifted or crackled beneath their weight.

"Did we lose him?" Stefani whispered.

"I hope so," Robbie said. "There's an opening ahead. Let's get out of here."

One by one, they crept out into another clearing. Stefani came out last, head bowed forward, combing the sticks and leaves from her hair. "Do you think he's coming back?" she asked in a low voice.

"I think we can count on it." Robbie nudged her in the side.

She stopped brushing at her hair with her fingers and looked up. "Oh."

Before them, ranged in a circle, was an entire flight of fireworms. The stench of their fiery breath wafted off them as twenty pairs of angry yellow eyes glared at the party of travelers.

"Sssso pleasssant of you to join ussssss," Longscar said, landing before them with an awkward thud.

***

Stefani gripped her walking stick, her knuckles white with the pressure. Robbie held his knife. Their weapons were ridiculous against an entire flight of fireworms, but it made Stefani feel better to know they had something they could use to fight with. She just hoped it wouldn't come to that. "What do you want?"

Longscar jutted his head forward on his thick neck. His hot stinking breath washed over her and Stefani gagged. "What we want issss what we were promissssed," Longscar said. "Peasssse and prosssssperity." He swung his head from Stefani to Robbie. "Can you give usss that?"

"We don't even know what that means," Robbie said.

Sealeaf frowned and moved her hands quickly. *I know.*

"Really?" Stefani asked.

Sealeaf nodded, her hands moving a bit more slowly.

*Peace and a share of the-*there was a word Stefani couldn't understand-*of Anoria.*

"Oooh," Ranya said.

"What does that mean?" Robbie asked.

"When the king promised them a share in the prosperity of the land, they expected, well, plenty of food and everything. And, instead, this is what they have." Ranya held out her hands to take in the dying forest. "What all of us have," she said pointedly. "It's like this everywhere. Not just here," she told Longscar.

"We care only how it issss for ussss." Longscar slithered closer.

"What is it you expect us to do about it?" Stefani asked.

"Make. It. Right." Longscar stuck his ugly maw right in her face. She held her breath and leaned away.

The other fireworms flapped their wings and hissed in agreement.

"That's what we're trying to do," Robbie said. "And we'd be closer to getting it done if you hadn't stopped us."

The fireworms hissed again, but this time it didn't sound like approval.

"What sort of tricksss are you up to, thisss time? How much more damage will you caussse?" Longscar demanded. "You have already ruined the land. What more do you wisssh to do?"

"We didn't ruin it," Robbie said hotly, but Stefani felt her stomach lurch.

There it was again. This was all her fault. Trapping the Greatstone in the land had done something horrible to the magic. Something she wasn't sure they could undo. But they needed to try. They needed to save Laurel. But how could they do anything with these creatures barring the way? "We're on a quest," she said with as much confidence as she could muster. "For Laurel Silverbark." Not exactly a lie. Stefani turned the ring around on her finger. "She brought us here. She sent us to . . . to find a magic . . .

um, talisman that will fix the magic and restore the land."

Robbie stared at her for a moment, and she gave him a wide-eyed look. He nodded. "Yup. Talisman."

The fireworms swayed back and forth, sighing, whistling, and belching. It sounded like an argument between a steam locomotive and a roomful of boiling teakettles.

Longscar slithered back to the circle of fireworms and began hissing louder than ever, drowning out the rest of them. Finally, he turned back to Stefani and Robbie. "We have reached an agreement." He swayed back and forth, indicating the crowd of fireworms behind him. "We will give you a chance to fix thingssss as you say." He swung his head forward. "But one of you mussst remain here with ussss. One of you mussst be our hosssstage. And if you sshould fail to return the prosssperity we dessserve." He belched a burst of fire at them and they jumped back. "Hossstage becomesss sacrifice!"

"No." Stefani waved her hand in front of her face to wave away Longscar's foul stench. Her face felt singed and, with nervous fingers, she reached up to make sure she still had her eyebrows. "We can't leave anyone behind. We need everyone." She let her hand drop.

"That's right," Robbie chimed in. "We're a special team. We were chosen for this quest because we each have, um, special skills we're going to need to complete it."

"You'll jussst have to find a way to do without sssome of thosssse skilssss, then." Longscar told them. "Thisss isss not up for dissscusssion. Choose."

Robbie and Stefani shook their heads.

"Chooossse," Longscar commanded, smoke rising from his nostrils. Behind him, the other fireworms writhed, erupting in angry hisses and ugly burbles.

Sealeaf tapped Stefani on the elbow and pointed to herself. "No!" Stefani yelped.

Sealeaf stamped her foot insistently and pointed again to herself.

"Stefani's right. We . . . we . . . just can't do that," Robbie said.

"Choossse! Or all will burn!" Longscar reared back and gulped in air, preparing to spit fire at them.

Sealeaf made a quick series of insistent hand gestures.

Ranya tugged at Stefani's collar. "Sealeaf is right," the Lightwing murmured in her ear. "You need to choose her to stay behind."

Stefani opened her mouth in an "O" of understanding. "Fine," she told Longscar. "Her." She pointed at Sealeaf.

"What?" Robbie stared at her in alarm. "You can't be serious."

"I am," Stefani said firmly. She looked back at the fireworms surrounding them. "She's the only one whose, um, skills, we can do without. It's her or us." She crossed her arms as the fireworms rumbled and hissed in satisfaction. All except Longscar who seemed disappointed. "But no harm can come to her," Stefani told the fireworms, "or we will send the sorceress after you." She stared hard at them, giving them what her mom referred to as her award-winning death glare.

Longscar snorted. "Termsss are oursss to set, but pile of assssh makesss no good hossstage." He eyed the young Glimmering. "Sssacrificesss, though . . ."

Robbie was still looking at Stefani as if she'd suddenly eaten some kid's pet gerbil.

"We got it," Stefani huffed. "One order of peace and prosperity coming up." She stalked off, forcing herself not to look back until she reached the trees.

Robbie planted his feet. "I'm staying, too."

With a quick movement, Sealeaf signaled him to go.

"I'm not leaving you here alone. With them." He stepped closer to her.

Without warning, she shoved him so hard, he lost his balance and had to pinwheel his arms to keep from falling. Then she turned her back and stepped closer to the line of bobbing, wriggling fireworms, refusing to look at him.

The fireworms hissed in laughter.

"Robbie, come on," Stefani urged through clenched teeth.

"Fine. You're all crazy, but whatever." Robbie turned and stomped after Stefani and Ranya.

CHAPTER TWENTY-TWO

"Sshhhh," Ranya whispered.

"We didn't make a sound," insisted Robbie, still unhappy about the entire plan. What if something went wrong? "This is a bad idea. What if we can't sneak Sealeaf away from the fireworms?"

"If you had another plan, you should have said so at the time," Stefani whispered back, pulling up handfuls of brittle moss.

"No one gave me a chance to say anything."

"We couldn't very well talk about it out loud in front of Longscar and his team of nasties," Stefani told him.

"Well, there should have been something else we could have done besides leaving her with those jerks."

"Sshhhh," Ranya hushed them again. "You're already

too big and loud without all the talking. Besides, there's no way to unset the sun."

"What?" Robbie said.

"She means, you can't turn back the clock," Stefani murmured. "We just have to move forward. Sealeaf is depending on us."

"I know," grumbled Robbie, wishing he'd been able to fight Longscar face-to-face. But even without an entire flight of fireworms backing their enemy, there was no way for two kids, a Lightwing, and a Glimmering to take him on. Bullies! That's what Longscar and his brood were. "I hate bullies." Ever since he'd finally stood up to Freddy after their last trip to Anoria, he'd made it a point not to back down from a bully. Now this. "And I hate that we don't have a better plan."

"Ranya says this moss will do the trick," Stefani said. "We just need to gather enough of it, then get close enough to spread it around outside their den."

Robbie looked at the curling yellow-brown leaves in his hand. "I still don't see how it's going to do much good." He raised his hand to his nose and sniffed.

"Don't!" Ranya dive-bombed between him and the wad of moss in his hands.

"I was just trying to see if it smelled," Robbie said, scratching at his nose with the back of his hand.

"Have you ever had poison oak or poison ivy?" Stefani asked him.

"Yeah. Once. It sucked." He wriggled his itchy nose.

Ranya shook her head. "You got some in your nose, didn't you?"

"What?" Robbie smushed his nose against his shoulder. "This stuff isn't doing a thing to my bare hands."

"That's because it only causes a reaction when it comes into contact with mucous membranes," Stefani said. "Like your nose and—"

"Oh!" Robbie dropped the pile of moss he'd collected

and pinched his nose shut between his finger and thumb. "Great. This is gonna drive me nuts!"

"Well, at least we know it works." Stefani picked up the moss he'd dropped and added it to her stack. Then she used the heel of her hiking boot to grind the dried moss against the flat stone they'd found. "Now, all we have to do is figure out a delivery system."

"Wait here. I have an idea." Ranya zipped away into the nearby trees.

"This should totally get them focused on something else." Robbie gritted his teeth against the horrible itch making its way deeper into his head.

Ranya returned, carrying a tight-knit mesh made of fine threads. "Spider webbing," she told them, spreading the fabric out.

"Where did you get it?" Stefani asked.

"It normally takes days to gather enough webbing and spin it into cloth for a net like this." Ranya patted her sword and started loading the ground-up moss into the bag. "I managed to convince a few local spiders it was in their best interest to help."

"Here, let me do that," Robbie offered, mashing his nose into his shoulder to keep from sneezing. "My hands are bigger, so it'll go faster. Besides, I'm already infected with the stuff."

Ranya nodded and flew up to an overhead branch to supervise the filling of the net.

"So, even if we do manage to distract the guard without getting burned to a cinder, how do we get them to crawl through this stuff?" Robbie rubbed his nose. "I mean, don't you think they know this stuff is bad for them?"

"Now that it's crushed up, we can spread it in the dirt," Ranya told them. "If I do my part well enough, they won't know it's there until it's too late."

"Okay," Robbie said. "But let's hope by the time it starts to work, it's not too late for us."

"That's full enough," Ranya said. "If I try and carry too much, I won't be able to fly well enough to dodge their flames."

Robbie pulled the ends of the silken material together to form a pouch and helped Ranya loop the ends over her shoulders.

"Hand me that line right there," Ranya said as she hovered in the air in front of them. "But be careful," she warned. "That's my quick release cord. Once it's pulled the cloth opens and spills out the powdered moss. Wouldn't want you getting another dose."

Being super-careful, Robbie handed her the end of the loose thread. "I still think this is bad idea."

"It's the best tactic under the circumstances," Ranya told him.

"That doesn't mean I have to like it."

"I understand," the Lightwing told him. "No good soldier likes to be left on the sideline, but sometimes it is necessary."

Robbie's cheeks warmed, but he could only nod.

"Wish me luck." Ranya buzzed her wings.

"Good luck," Stefani said.

Robbie stifled a sneeze and held up crossed fingers as Ranya flew out of the open space with her load of moss.

They worked in silence for a while, gathering more of the moss, piling it up in small heaps that would be just right for filling Ranya's silk carrying sack.

"I really hope this works." Robbie wiped at his nose again and again.

"You're going to rub it raw," Stefani said, continuing to work.

"I know," he told her, "but I can't help it. It itches like crazy."

"As much as I hate to say it, that's probably a good thing for us." Stefani pulled more moss off the base of a big tree and added it to their growing pile.

"Gee, thanks. So glad to be a successful guinea pig."

Stefani huffed out a small laugh. "I didn't tell you to stick your nose in the stuff."

"I know. I know," Robbie said. "Sorry."

"Maybe Ranya knows where to find an antidote."

"Or maybe Sealeaf does," Robbie said.

"Sure. That makes sense. Glimmering know a ton of forest stuff." Stefani pried another patch of moss free from the tree. "We can ask her as soon as we rescue her."

"Or we could just ask her now," Robbie suggested.

"Right. Hahaha. Not funny, Robbie."

"I'm serious," he said.

Stefani stopped what she was doing and turned. Sealeaf stood beside her, a sneaky smile lighting up her face.

"How?"

Sealeaf shrugged.

A fierce screech erupted from the direction of the fireworm den at the same time as Ranya burst through the trees. "Time to go," she said, leading the way.

"But what about the rest of the moss?" Stefani said.

"I don't think we'll be needing it now," Ranya yelled over her shoulder.

Stefani dropped the clump of moss she'd been holding and ran.

Robbie followed behind, rubbing at his nose. "You mean I got that stuff up my nose for nothing?"

"Not exactly for nothing," Ranya called back to him "Let's just say that when I saw how long it was going to take to spread that stuff far enough around to make a rescue possible, your accidental dosing gave me the idea to spill some into their watering hole."

"What will that do?" Stefani asked.

"Apparently, besides causing horrible mouth itching, it upsets their stomachs." Ranya told them.

"So?"

"Have you ever seen a fire-spitting monster sneeze and

burp at the same time?"

A sudden flash illuminated the forest behind them, followed by another and another, all accompanied by a lot of loud screeches and angry hissing.

"Ohhhh," Stefani said.

Robbie grinned as they ran through the forest, picturing the band of angry fireworms uncontrollably belching fire at one another. "That's going to hurt."

"Let's hope it keeps them busy for a while," Ranya said.

CHAPTER TWENTY-THREE

The day drew on toward afternoon as they struggled up the rocky path. Their narrow escape the night before from the angry fireworms had kept them on the move, afraid to rest for too long. Sleeping had been out of the question. Now, exhausted, they trudged uphill, fighting the brisk winds that had risen as they'd climbed out of the forest.

"Are you sure this is the way?" Stefani asked.

"Neither Sealeaf nor I know any other way across." Ranya shouted to be heard, her words sweeping up and away on the wind. She clung to the lip of the side pocket of Stefani's pack. She'd refused to climb in at first but, after being whipped away from her perch on Stefani's shoulder one too many times, had finally agreed. Though, she'd insisted that Stefani leave the flap unsnapped.

The higher they climbed, the more the wind buffeted them. They stayed close to the rocky cliff that rose upward on one side, steering clear of the long drop on the other. Stefani kept one hand against the cliff to keep from being battered into the rocky surface. It was like fighting against an avalanche of air. The gusting wind kicked up dust and dirt that scratched and scraped at them, as if alive and angry to have strangers trespassing here.

"Is it always like this?" Robbie had to yell to be heard over the whistling and screaming wind that poured down on them through the pass.

Sealeaf tapped Robbie on the shoulder to get his attention and made several quick gestures.

Robbie shook his head. "I'm sorry," he said. "I still don't understand."

Sealeaf tilted her head to one side and frowned. She dropped her hands in frustration, turned, and began pushing her way against the wind, once more.

Stefani trudged up the hill to stand beside him. She watched Sealeaf moving away from them. "Is she okay?" Her raised voice was muffled behind the bandanna she had tied around her face like some kind of bank robber.

"I think she's tired of trying to communicate and not getting through," he hollered back. "You and Ranya seem to understand her pretty well, but I just can't get the hang of it." The wind buffeted them as they stood together struggling to keep their balance.

Stefani stared after Sealeaf for a moment. "It just takes time to learn a new language."

"Yeah, sure. I guess." Robbie pulled his t-shirt back up over his nose and mouth. He put his head down and followed behind her.

They struggled against the harsh wind for another half hour or more.

"How much farther?" Stefani had to pull her bandanna away from her face and shout to be heard over the howling gale. Dirt and leaves attacked her face and the swirling dust filled her mouth. She quickly pulled the bandanna back into place.

Sealeaf shrugged.

Stefani put her head down and pushed into the wind.

Robbie leaned forward as a great gust of wind slammed into him and shoved him back. Then, just as quickly as it had started, it died down, and he stumbled forward onto his knees. Before Stefani could move, Sealeaf helped him up.

His t-shirt slipped down from his face as he stood. "Thank you!" he shouted as the wind once more returned to a screaming gale.

Sealeaf put her fingertips just below her lips and pulled her hand away.

Robbie stared at Sealeaf and she repeated the gesture.

"What's she saying?" Robbie hollered.

"I think it means you're welcome," Stefani called back.

Sealeaf tilted her head to one side. She tapped Robbie on the shoulder, pointed to his mouth, and made the gesture again.

"No," he said. "It means 'thank you.'" He put his hand to his lips and pulled it away, mimicking Sealeaf's motion.

The Glimmering nodded her approval. With her palm up, she made a circle from her heart out and back again.

"I guess that means 'you're welcome.'" Robbie said, trying out the movement. "Cool."

The corners of Sealeaf's mouth quirked up into smile. Then she ducked her head, tucking her chin in and wrapping her headscarf around her face in a single fluid movement. She turned and led them forward into the blasting wind.

CHAPTER TWENTY-FOUR

When they finally reached the top of the pass and started down the other side, the wind grew less fierce. By the time they neared the bottom, it had slowed to a mild breeze. Ranya ducked outside of the safety of the pocket and climbed up onto Stefani's shoulder. She clung tight to the strap of Stefani's backpack. "Even here the plants are dying." She eyed the withered trees and the parched-looking plants. "The sickness has truly affected our entire world."

Stefani pushed her bandanna down so it hung around her neck. "It's like nowhere in Anoria is safe from this awfulness. I'm so sorry."

Ahead of them, Sealeaf paused, then came running back to them, waving her arms excitedly.

"What is it?" Robbie asked.

She turned and pointed, signing in short, rapid movements.

"I'm not sure. It's too fast," Ranya said. "But it's something important."

Sealeaf threw up her hands in frustration, gestured for them to follow her and ran ahead.

They hurried to catch up and found her in an open meadow, kneeling over what appeared to be a patch of freshly wilted flowers.

Ranya leaped from Stefani's shoulder and swooped down for a closer look. "You're right," she said, as Sealeaf gestured and pointed. "These were fresh and green not too long ago. What do you think? A day?"

Sealeaf wiggled her hand to signal more or less.

"I agree," Ranya told her. "That means something is fighting the sickness here. But what could it be?"

Sealeaf pointed at her eyes and then gestured outward.

"Yes. We should search for more signs. Maybe we can find a cure." Ranya suddenly sounded hopeful.

Stefani watched the exchange in fascination. Surprisingly, she had followed most of what Sealeaf was saying, without Ranya interpreting.

"All right," Robbie said. "We should split up. We can cover more ground that way, but I think we should stay within sight of one another. There's no telling what might be out here."

"Agreed." Stefani hefted her walking stick and headed left. The others set off in different directions.

A few paces away, Stefani came upon another wilted plant. This one had flowered before dropping its petals and slumping over. The stem was still green and flexible. A short distance away, she spotted another. Then another. And another. She followed the trail of plants, stopping suddenly when she realized she'd just traveled in a circle.

"Hey!" she called out to the others.

"What's up?" Robbie called. "Did you find something?"

"I'm not sure." Stefani retraced her steps, walking around the circle of plants. "But this is really strange."

The others joined her and surveyed the circle of wilted plants.

Sealeaf knelt beside one of the plants, brushing her fingertips over the grass that grew around the base of the stem. She waved Stefani over and pointed at the ground.

Squatting low to get a better look, Stefani almost toppled over when she saw how green the shoots of grass were. "It's like it just grew."

Nodding, Sealeaf pointed again. There, filled with freshly sprouted grass was the outline of a footprint. A human print and, judging by the size, from someone big. "Can you tell how long ago?" Stefani asked, as Robbie and Ranya examined the print.

Sealeaf held up a finger, then pointed at the sun.

"A day?"

Sealeaf shook her head, then made a chopping motion at her finger.

"Less than a day?"

Sealeaf nodded again.

Ranya sailed up to Stefani's shoulder. "Hard to tell with the way things wither and die since the sickness set in, but I agree. Less than a day."

"But what does it mean?" Robbie asked. "Do we keep going? Or do we try and find what's causing the plants to suddenly grow and die?"

"This might be the cure for the sickness. It might save all our people. We should follow the trail," Ranya said. "Sealeaf and I can track them."

The Glimmering nodded in agreement, her eyes alight with excitement.

Stefani chewed her lip and spun the silver band on her finger. The image of Laurel standing deathly still in Aurien's Glen rose before her. Changing direction now was a risk.

Laurel needed the Awakener. But the land needed a cure. She gazed at Ranya and Sealeaf, realizing how important this could be to them and their people. It could mean the difference between life and...She left that thought alone. Anyway, if they found a cure, maybe it could help Laurel, too. "I think it's worth it to see if we can find whoever is causing this."

Robbie nodded. "I'm in."

Ranya leaped into the air. "Come on Sealeaf. Let's get tracking."

Together, the Lightwing and Glimmering set off. Ranya zipped forward and Sealeaf scanned the ground ahead. They followed the trail of footprints and wilted flowers.

"You sure you're good with this?" Robbie asked, cupping a hand over his eyes and gazing after their companions.

"I think we should give Ranya and Sealeaf the chance to track the person who left these." Stefani pointed to the plants and the prints. "They deserve the opportunity to help their people. But if we don't find who caused this by sundown..."

"Okay." Robbie hiked his pack up onto his shoulders. They set off after Ranya and Sealeaf.

CRRR
RRCR

CHAPTER TWENTY-FIVE

Evening threatened to catch them. The sun drew lower and lower in the sky as they threaded their way through forest and fields, following the trail of wilted flowers and small patches of fast-fading grass. Ranya would exclaim in excitement when they discovered an especially recent growth, or a tree that seemed to have sprouted fresh leaves. But then the trail would fade again. The wilted plants dried out, the grass grew yellow, and there was still no sign of who or what they were tracking.

The trail led them in a meandering pattern, sometimes circling around and bringing them back to a place they had already been. More than once, Ranya and Sealeaf paused, communicating what was clearly frustration. But each time, they would search until they found another trail of newly withered plants.

Robbie paused a short distance from a large tree that had once been noble and tall. Now, it bowed low, trailing dead branches along the ground. He called out to the others. "I think we should stop for the night. This tree should give us good cover and there's plenty of wood to make a fire."

Stefani sighed and slipped off her backpack, heading toward the tree. She stopped suddenly, and backed up a step.

"What is it?" Robbie said, warily. He quickened his pace, then stopped beside her when he saw what she was gaping at.

The tree branches that from a distance had appeared completely dead, were covered in tiny green buds. And beneath them lay an old man with bare feet and a long white beard. He wore a patchwork robe and was sound asleep, curled on his side, snoring. Bright green blades of grass surrounded him, as if he'd been unable to resist the fresh patch of new growth and had lain down to rest. Deep in sleep, he seemed unaware of them.

"Do you think he's dangerous?" Stefani whispered as she backed away from the tree and the sleeping man.

Robbie stared at the old man without answering.

She turned to him. "Robbie?"

He took a step back, his stomach tight. What was an old guy like this doing out here? It wasn't right. Old people belonged in hospitals or assisted living facilities, places where someone could take care of them. Not out in the woods, sleeping under trees. He took another step back, tripping over a broken tree branch and falling backward. He landed with a thud.

"Robbie?" Stefani rushed over to him. "Are you okay?" She reached out her hand to help him.

That's it, he thought, I'll just take her hand and we'll go back.

But Stefani jerked her hand away at the last second.

"No. We have to stay and help."

"Sorry," Robbie mumbled. He stood up and brushed himself off, then pointed at the old man, who was now wide awake and staring at all of them. "But what do we do with him?"

CRED
ЄОCR

CHAPTER TWENTY-SIX

Stefani stared at the wizened man. He was older than anyone she had ever seen. A million wrinkles crisscrossed his ancient face. His pale blue eyes never quite seemed to focus on anything. And, as she stared at him, he hummed something under his breath. It was an odd little tune, at once both strange yet familiar and, as the music took shape, memories flowed inside her head. Childhood visions from many years ago, mixed with memories from recent weeks. Emotions shivered their way across her heart as she remembered past holidays, learning to ride a bike, her first taste of strawberry lemonade, the day she and Robbie had first come to Anoria. Each memory was as sharp and fresh as if it had just happened.

"Stef?"

She heard her name being called as if from far away. The voice pulled her out of the memories and brought her back.

"Stefani?"

She shook her head, trying to clear the last of the vivid recollections from her brain.

"Stef, are you okay?" Robbie stood beside her, looking worried.

"Yeah." She gazed around her, slowly remembering where she was. "I...I'm good."

"Your thoughts seemed to be elsewhere," Ranya said.

"I guess I kind of got lost in my head for a minute," Stefani said. The taste of fresh lemonade lingered on her tongue.

Sealeaf gestured to her head and then pointed to the old man, who sat on the ground before them, his legs pulled up, chin resting on his knees. He stroked his beard and stared at them, as if not really seeing them.

Robbie took a step toward him. "What did you do to her?" he demanded, fists clenching.

The old man looked up, as if just seeing them. "Good day." He stood abruptly, and bowed low, his beard sweeping the ground before him. "A pleasure to meet you. Indeed. A fine pleasure."

Robbie's mouth fell open.

Ranya buzzed around the old man, examining him from every angle. "No weapons. He seems harmless."

He watched her, turning in a circle to follow her flight, one fist gripping a handful of his long beard. He grinned. "Oh, pretty!"

"Ranya," Stefani said. "You're going to make him dizzy."

The Lightwing zipped over to light on Stefani's shoulder.

The old man let go of his beard, stuck his arms out and continued to spin in a circle, laughing. After a moment, the laughter turned to a cough. He stopped spinning and bent over, placing his hands on his knees and panting. "Not so young, now." He coughed again. "Late in the year? So much turning, turning, turning."

"Yes," agreed Stefani. "I think you may have done too much spinning."

The old man glanced up at her sharply, then over at Robbie, and back at her. "Oh, I see. Yes, of course. Of course. The threads of weft and weave."

Stefani had no idea what he was talking about, and his bright red face worried her.

She opened her water bottle and held it out to him. "Here," she said. "Some water might help."

He eyed the bottle, then stood up and took the water from her. He held the bottle up in the late afternoon sunlight, then peered down inside. Then he held the bottle above his face and leaned his head back, pouring water into his mouth until it cascaded down his chin and neck. It splashed down his front, wetting the long robe he wore. He held the water in his mouth for a moment, pushing his cheeks out like a chipmunk. Then he swallowed and handed the almost empty bottle back. He let out a large belch, then promptly sat down on the ground and began petting the flowers that had bloomed at his feet.

"We should go," Robbie shook his head. "This guy is crazy."

"But shouldn't we help him?" Stefani capped the nearly empty water bottle before putting it away.

"What do you want us to do?" Robbie asked, his voice sharp. "Find him a nice nursing home to move into?"

"Well, no," Stefani said, slowly. "But I don't think we should leave him out here all alone. Do you?"

"Stefani," Robbie said. "Look around. It's not like we can just call 9-1-1 and have them send an ambulance or something."

"I know that."

"What's 9-1-1?" Ranya asked.

"It's an emergency number you can call in our world when someone is in trouble," Stefani explained.

The old man stood up. "Goodness. Is someone in trouble? What kind of trouble?"

Robbie shook his head. "Seriously?"

"If someone is in trouble, we must help them." The old man's face wrinkled with concern. "Trouble. Trouble. Not good. Terrible. Terrible. Rotten fruit."

"It's fine. Everyone is just fine. No one is in trouble." Stefani took the old man by the arm soothingly.

Sealeaf gestured frantically for their attention.

"What?" Ranya huffed.

Sealeaf pointed to the old man's feet where the grass was now lush and green and more flowers had sprung up.

Stefani dropped the man's thin arm and took a step

back. "Is it him? Is he what's causing the plants to grow again?"

Where the old man had been sitting, and all around where he now stood, grass sprouted and flowers grew. They budded and bloomed, opening bright petals of every color, like time-lapse photography.

"He could be the cure," Ranya said, excitedly.

"I don't know," Robbie said. "Seems like all he's able to do is wake stuff up for a short time. Then, it all starts dying again. Not much of a cure, if you ask me."

"I suppose you're right," Ranya said, the excitement draining from her voice.

Sealeaf signed something and pointed at the old man.

"Wait." Stefani stiffened. "What did you say?"

Sealeaf gestured again.

"Not that. Robbie, what did you just say about what he does?"

"I said, all he seems to do is wake stuff-—"

"Exactly," Stefani said. "You don't think he's…"

Robbie shook his head. "No. It's not possible. He can't be—"

Stefani stared at the old man before them in wonder.

Sealeaf nodded her head vigorously and signed, *I've been trying to tell you.*

"Really?" Ranya buzzed closer to peer into the old man's face. He held out a hand to make her a seat. The Lightwing hesitated. "Are you sure?"

The old man grinned and winked at her. Then he reached over and plucked a dead twig from the nearby tree. Cupping the twig between his hands, he closed his eyes, then let out a small giggle of glee. He opened his hands to reveal a red blossom with a base that looked like a fat sack filled to bursting.

Ranya let out a small yelp of excitement, then dove forward. "Sweet blossom!?!" She landed on the old man's wrinkled palm beside the flower and shoved her tiny hand inside, scooping out a rich orange liquid. She held her cupped hand up to her face and sniffed, her eyes closing in delight. Then she slurped the liquid off her fingers and reached for more.

Eyes wide, Stefani turned to Robbie. "Well, that's a surprise."

Robbie stood frozen.

Ranya finished off her feast and licked her fingers clean. "We've not had fresh sweet blossom in more than a turn. I can travel for days on that." She rose into the air, wings buzzing.

Sealeaf wrinkled her nose in distaste.

"Ah," the Awakener said. "Far away begins the day." He reached behind his back with his empty hands, then brought his fists out in front of him, offering them to Sealeaf. The Glimmering tilted her head to the side in a questioning manner.

"I think he wants you to pick one," Stefani said.

Sealeaf glanced at her, then took a step closer to the old man. Slowly, she pointed to his left hand.

He opened it, but it was empty. Sealeaf frowned.

The Awakener wiggled his other hand until she pointed to it. When he opened it, a handful of brown nuts spilled out. Sealeaf smiled and took the nuts from his hand, then gathered the ones that had fallen onto the ground.

"Those were Gamdol's favorite," Robbie said.

Stefani stared at the old man who was now bending down to sniff the bright new blooms at his feet. "He's the one we're looking for."

Robbie shook his head. "It can't be him. He can't be the—"

"The Awakener!" Ranya and Stefani chorused.

CHAPTER TWENTY-SEVEN

Robbie led the way, with Stefani behind him. He walked as far from the old man as possible. "He makes me uncomfortable," he told Stefani, refusing to admit to himself there was more to it than that.

"He's just old." Stefani said.

"He's not just old," Robbie shot back. "He's crazy. Just look at him. His clothes are on backward and the colors don't even match and he doesn't make any sense. And...he just bugs me."

Robbie eyed the Awakener, who had plopped down onto the ground. He sat cross-legged, examining a trail of ants that marched across the path and off into the grass.

"He's wearing a robe. How can you tell if it's on backward or frontward?" Stefani said.

Robbie turned away. "Whatever."

The old man was humming again, another tuneless song that repeated over and over.

"Fine." Stefani handed Robbie her compass. "You take the lead. I'll walk back here with him. Let's just hurry and get back to Laurel."

The Awakener was now crawling on his hands and knees, following the ants on their march. "Come on," Stefani said, helping him to stand. "Time to go."

The old man looked around in wonder. "Time? Time! When are we?" he asked.

Robbie rolled his eyes. "Good luck with that." He laid the compass on the palm of his hand and purposely ignored them.

"Oh, shiny." The Awakener reached for the compass, but Robbie swatted his hand away.

"Ow." The Awakener pulled his hand back and petted his fingers.

"Robbie!" Stefani scolded.

"Would you rather I let him break it?" Robbie said, but his stomach churned at the thought of what he'd just done. Then the guilt turned to anger. Why did the old guy have to be such a pain?

"No, but you didn't have to be so mean about it." Stefani frowned at him.

The Awakener wrapped his fingers together, then placed his hands beneath his chin and hunched over them. He gave Robbie a thoughtful look.

Robbie knew he was being unreasonable, but he couldn't help it. "He's just so aggravating."

"He doesn't mean to be." Stefani reached up to put a hand on the old man's shoulder and he flinched away from her. "It's okay," she murmured. "He didn't mean it."

Robbie shoved the compass into his pocket. "Whatever."

"You should try to at least be nice to him. It isn't like he can help being the way he is."

"I know." Robbie refused to look at her. In a way, he felt bad for the old guy. "It's just..."

Just then, the Awakener let out a startled gasp and Robbie clamped his mouth shut again. "What now?"

The Awakener walked in a circle. Each place he stepped, the ground turned green and flowers budded. He followed the greenery, trying to pick the blooms that sprang up along the path where he'd walked. Only, the tiny flowers faded before he could reach them. So, he kept going, following his own blooming footsteps in an ever-widening circle.

"Hey," Robbie called. "Hey, you! Stop that. We need to get going." But the Awakener seemed unaware of anything but the plants growing in his wake.

Sealeaf watched in fascination, a look of awe on her face.

"Can you please do something about that?" Robbie pointed at the old man, who was still walking in circles, oohing and aahing at the new life that had sprung from beneath his feet. "This guy is nuts. How is he going to help if we can't even get him to walk in a straight line?" He heard how grumpy the words came out, but he didn't care. He'd come to Anoria to get away from this kind of stuff. And here he was having to deal with it anyway. It wasn't fair!

Ranya fluttered overhead, attempting to get the Awakener's attention. The old man only sighed with sadness as each petal and leaf turned brown before he could bend down to examine them more closely.

"Fine. I'll take care of it. Playing peacekeeper between you two is going to be a full-time job." Stefani walked over to the Awakener's side and touched his arm. "Now, I get what my mom means when she says she doesn't get paid enough for this kind of stuff."

The old man started. He clasped his hands to his chest and hunched his shoulders. His pale blue eyes went wide and he stared at her. He blinked several times, as if he was trying to remember something. Then his face cleared and his eyes turned a brilliant sky blue. "Your friend is trapped. She needs our help. You must take me to her. Quickly."

Robbie started to reply, then stopped.

The old man's eyes had faded back to pale blue again. He bowed his head and looked down at his feet. "Oooh." His long beard fluffing as his lips curved into a smile. "Lovely."

Robbie's gaze followed his. Green vines tangled themselves around the Awakener's feet, twining around his calves.

Rainbow hued flowers budded and bloomed from the vines. Instead of facing the sun, as flowers normally do, each blossom turned its face toward Stefani. It was as if they were staring at her...

Stefani took a step back. "We...we need to go," she said in a low voice. "We need to go now."

Robbie wasn't sure exactly what had just happened. Or why. But it had sure spooked her. "Stef, what . . ."

The Awakener shuffled forward. The vines fell away from him, fading and turning to dust with a quiet whisper.

Stefani glanced over at Robbie. Her face had lost all its color. He took a step toward her, but she shook her head.

The old man set off, muttering under his breath as he passed them. "Things are always complicated at the start. Difficult before done, easier after."

CHAPTER TWENTY-EIGHT

Going back up the mountain took a lot more time with the Awakener in tow. Robbie led the way, clutching the compass. He really wanted to talk to Stefani. After all, they had come on this journey together. Only now . . . all her attention was on the crazy old guy, and Robbie didn't much want to hang around *him*.

Robbie paused to wait in the shade of a rock ledge. He set his pack down on the path and wiped his forehead with his forearm. He was covered in dust, and so were his clothes. A dark brown smirch stained his shirt where he'd been using it to wipe away the sweat. The others were taking forever to catch up. He gritted his teeth to keep from telling them to hurry up.

On the trail below, Stefani panted, her breathing ragged

from exertion. She and Sealeaf took turns gently pushing and pulling the Awakener up the steep path. The old man shuffled forward at a constant pace. A snail's pace, Robbie thought. No, make that slower than a snail. He shook his head and took a drink of water. He sloshed the warm liquid around in his mouth before swallowing, then recapped the bottle. They needed to make their supplies last. There were five of them now, and they hadn't seen a stream or rivulet for miles.

Ranya flew up beside him and looked back. Stefani struggled with the old man, who twirled his long beard like a ribbon as they hiked up the steep path. "He is not what I expected." She landed on Robbie's pack.

Robbie snorted. "No kidding. He's slower than a slug crawling backward."

"The wolf slugs were faster than that." Ranya pointed at the Awakener, who had made a sudden U-turn and was trying to head back down the path while Sealeaf and Stefani struggled to get him pointed back in the right direction. "At least they were focused."

Robbie thought about their encounter with the huge, slimy creatures. "Okay, not a good comparison. Bigger problem, the wind on the other side of the pass is going to blow us all the way down that side of the mountain. And he doesn't look too sturdy." He pointed up. The dark clouds that had scudded across the sky all day, gathered overhead. "Not to mention those clouds look like they're getting ready to do some serious raining."

Ranya scowled. "Oh, nettles!"

"What?" Robbie asked.

"I don't wish to ride inside that pocket, again." Her features softened as she looked down the path at the Awakener. "And I think you're right. He's going to continue to need a lot of help, even if the weather remains dry."

When they finally reached the shaded patch, Stefani helped the Awakener sit on a small boulder to rest. Then she slipped off her pack and sat down roughly. Sealeaf stayed beside the Awakener, watching him, eyes wide in wonder.

"How much farther to the top?" Stefani shielded her eyes against the sun to look up at Robbie.

"Not sure." Robbie kicked the ground with the toe of his boot, raising a cloud of dust.

"Thanks a lot." Stefani waved the dirt away with her hand.

Robbie felt a sliver of guilt and opened his mouth to apologize.

"Hello!" The Awakener wiggled his fingers in the dust motes that floated out of the shade, dancing in the sunlight.

"Stop that." Robbie's voice was sharper than he'd intended.

"Robbie," Stefani said, "can't you at least *try* to be nice to him?" She pulled out her water bottle and offered the Awakener a drink.

"He always does that."

"He always does what?"

The old man accepted the bottle and then tilted it up before putting it to his mouth. Water spilled onto his chin and ran down the front of his robes as he drank thirstily.

"Stuff. Like that." Robbie stabbed his finger in the Awakener's direction. "We don't have an endless supply of water, you know."

Stefani gently took the bottle back from the Awakener. "It's not like he's doing it on purpose."

"Yeah. So what?" Robbie reached down and picked up his pack, hitching the straps up onto his shoulders. "That doesn't make it okay." He stalked off up the trail, eyes burning.

"Where are you going? We just got here and we need to rest," he heard Stefani call after him.

"To see how far away we are from the top," he shot back at her without slowing down. "And to get away from him," he added under his breath. A sudden gust of wind picked up his muttered words and carried them away.

CRES
SDR

CHAPTER TWENTY-NINE

The wind blew harder as they neared the top of the pass.
The clouds overhead darkened, turning the day gloomy.
Robbie stayed out ahead, his eyes focused on the trail.

A great gust of wind swept Ranya high up into the air.
She tucked her wings as the wind tumbled her over and
over. Finally, she broke free of the current. She let the wind
push her through the sky in a loop-de-loop, and dove back
down to eye level with Stefani.

The old man laughed gleefully, swooping his hand
through the air, following her flight path.

She hovered in front of Stefani and frowned, a look of
defeat on her face. "In the forest, we are protected from the
winds." She paused, wrinkling her forehead. "At least, we
used to be."

"I'm sorry it's not comfortable for you." Stefani reached back and held open her pack's side flap, allowing the Lightwing to slip inside the pocket.

"Thank you," Ranya said. "I should not complain."

"I understand. I'll try not to let it get too bumpy." She looked up just in time to see the Awakener once more heading back the way they had come. Sealeaf had hold of his robe, but the old man kept going, unaware he was dragging the Glimmering behind him.

"Whoa." Stefani called, jogging after them. She gently took him by the arm and guided him back toward the summit. "Sorry, Ranya." The poor Lightwing was getting that bumpy ride, after all.

To make matters worse, just as they reached the top of the pass, the clouds let loose dumping a ton of water on them. The Awakener looked up and smiled, tilting his head back and letting the rain fall in his face. "Life," he said and giggled like a child.

Robbie shook his head and turned away.

"We need a place to rest and wait out the storm," Stefani said, her wet hair already plastered against her head.

"Why? It's just life. Right?" Robbie grumbled.

"I know you have a problem with him. I get that he's acting all weird, like he's crazy or lost his mind or something, but we need to work together." Stefani wiped the rain out of her eyes.

"Or something?" Robbie mimicked. "Or something? We came all this way to find him. To get him to help. And instead, he's the one who needs help! He's got dementia, Stefani. That or Alzheimer's."

She glared at him.

"You know, dementia, when old people forget who they are and who everyone else is. And they can't remember what day it is. Or what they just did with their toothbrush." He wiped at his eyes. "He's sick and messed up and he's not going to get any better!"

"I know what it means," Stefani said in a quiet voice. "But he can't help it. And neither can your grandfather."

Robbie's face crumpled. "Don't you think I know that?"

Stefani shook her head. Rain dripped from her hair. "I think you need to give him, give them both, a break," she said softly. "And yourself, too."

"What?"

"You're angry, but I don't think it's at him. I think you're angry at yourself, for not knowing how to deal with it." She bit her lip. "When my dad left, my mom went through this period where she didn't want to do anything. She was tired all the time, hardly got out of bed some days." She looked down at her feet, then back up at Robbie. "She was depressed. I didn't know. I didn't understand. I was just angry. All the time. I thought I was just mad at *them*." She paused. "Then, I realized, I was mostly angry at me. I blamed myself. For not being able to fix it. Fix them." She shook her head. "There isn't anything you can do to fix it, Robbie. You can only do your best to remember him the way he was, and help him enjoy the times when he can remember, too."

"Stefani," Ranya said, peeking out from under the pocket flap. "He's going the wrong way again."

A short way down the trail, the Awakener splashed through a puddle.

With a sigh, Stefani ran after him.

CRCR
CRCR

CHAPTER THIRTY

Robbie stood there stunned. A rumble of thunder overhead mirrored the anger that welled inside him. Then, the clouds let loose another heavy torrent. With all the water running down his face, at least no one would be able to see he was crying. He wiped his face on his wet shirt, which didn't help.

After a minute, he pulled himself together. The others huddled beneath an overhanging boulder, trying to get out of the worst of the storm. The Awakener stood out in the rain, petting the rock as if it was some sort of large animal. A fresh pang of sorrow stabbed at Robbie's heart. No, he thought, he's not my grandfather. My grandfather still has some moments of awareness. He sometimes knows who I am. Sometimes, he even remembers when we used to play catch or hike, or go to the rock and gem show.

As the others huddled beside the boulder, the Awakener turned and looked him in the eye. The old man smiled, then waved and gestured for Robbie to come join them.

Slowly, as if walking to class for a test he hadn't studied for, Robbie slouched across the open space and joined the group. "I...I'm sorry, Stefani," he said, his ears hot despite the chilly rain. "I was—"

Sealeaf tugged at his shirt.

He glanced down to where she stared up at him with huge eyes. "Just a sec, okay? I really need to say..."

Sealeaf waved and pointed at the Awakener. Ranya peeked out from under the pocket flap.

Robbie turned in annoyance and his mouth fell open.

The old man stood with his arms stretched out, palms toward the ground, and all around him plants burst into existence. Vines grew and thrived. Flowers bloomed. Faded grass turned green. The tree beside them sent out buds that became leaves, then more buds that became flowers. It was like watching springtime in fast forward. The old man smiled, face raised to the sky. "Life," he said, his voice filled with joy.

Moss sprouted on the boulder and a rivulet of water trickled from it. The Awakener chuckled and nodded, petting the rock, once more. "Life."

"Fresh water!" Stefani grabbed a bottle and held it under the flow until it was full. Then she repeated the motion with another and another. Finally, she held out her hand to Robbie, who handed her his water bottles.

When their water bottles were filled, they took turns drinking from the clear water that spilled down the side of the mossy stone.

The Awakener grinned. Lush plants leaped to life all around them in a dazzling display. Robbie barely noticed when the rain slowed to a drizzle.

ೞಞ
ಞೞ

CHAPTER THIRTY-ONE

Once the rain let up, they continued over the summit
and headed down the other side. Shivering in their wet
clothes, they clung to the rocks to keep the blasting wind
from tumbling them over the cliff.

When they finally reached the bottom, the wind—which
had thankfully dried their clothes—died down, and the
clouds lifted. Ranya, relieved to be back out in the fresh
air, scouted ahead. Stefani kept a watchful eye on the
Awakener.

Sealeaf walked beside him, tugging at his sleeve when
he got distracted by a bug, or a leaf, or the flowers that
bloomed where he walked.

Once, when Stefani turned back to help, he looked up,
grinned and handed her a neat bundle of flowers. She held

the flowers in one hand and took his arm with the other. "We're going this way, now, Mr. Awakener."

He giggled and patted her hand, gazing at everything in wonder as if seeing the world for the first time as they walked. He grinned when Ranya flew up and landed on Stefani's shoulder. Then he stuck out his finger to stroke the Lightwing. Ranya cringed. Stefani worried the big man might forget his own strength and accidentally crush her wings. But his touch was as light as a hummingbird's feather, and his attention slipped away quickly.

"Stefani," Ranya said. "There's an open area off to the left up ahead. It will make a good place to stop and rest for the night."

"Okay," Stefani said, linking arms with the Awakener to guide him past a section of thorny bushes. "Let Robbie know we'll get there as soon as we can."

Ranya leaped backward off Stefani's shoulder and zipped away.

When they finally reached the wide space Ranya had described, Stefani was exhausted from herding the Awakener. The flowers he'd grown and picked for her had wilted in her fist. When he wasn't looking, she tossed them away and flexed her fingers to relieve the ache that had built up from clutching them.

Minding the Awakener wasn't an easy task, what with his constantly wandering focus. His eyes roved everywhere. And whatever his gaze landed on became the most fascinating thing in the world. He'd ooooh and aaaaah and reach out to touch and stroke leaves and branches, even briars. More than once, he'd been scratched or pricked on the finger by a thorn. But instead of crying out in pain, he only laughed and stuck his bloody finger in his mouth, watching with glee as the plant that had wounded him bloomed to health from his touch.

"I still don't understand how he's going to help," Robbie complained. "Even if we can get him to focus, things just die again once he walks away."

"I don't know," Stefanie told him, her own frustration showing. "Aurien thinks he can help, though. So, I'm going to make sure we bring him back to Laurel. Besides, you saw what he did in the rain. Maybe . . . maybe *those* plants are still blooming." She tried to sound more hopeful than she felt.

She could see how frustrating it might be for Robbie to be around someone who was so unfocused. Especially, if that person reminded you of someone who had once been a loving grandparent and now barely remembered you. She was becoming impatient, herself, worrying at the time it was taking to get back to Laurel. And they had no idea how much time the Treemage had. Another day? A few hours?

But she also found the Awakener to be kind of sweet with his childlike fascination with everything. Even his grinning and giggling could be infectious, and she found it impossible to stay frustrated when he pointed to an odd-shaped leaf or a winding tree limb that looked more like an elephant's trunk than a branch.

Beneath the long shadows of evening, she guided him to a rock in the clearing and helped him to sit, before helping Robbie and Sealeaf pile up dried brush and leaves for them all to sleep on.

"It's been getting kind of cold at night. You think we should gather firewood before it gets dark?" she asked.

Robbie surveyed the withered plants around them and shook his head. "Seems like a bad idea."

"Yeah, I guess you're right. Maybe if we pile up enough brush, we can use it to help keep ourselves warm."

Robbie stared thoughtfully at the Awakener, whose ankles had become wrapped in leafy vines just in the short time he'd been sitting still. "Sure." He went back to piling up dried plants for their bedding.

They ate the last of their granola bars. Robbie's stomach growled loud enough for Stefani to hear it, but there wasn't much they could do about it. They'd already eaten what they'd brought from home and most of the food Aurien had made them take. They'd tried to get the Awakener to grow more food, but he was often as likely to grow flowers or strange spiny plants.

After their sparse meal, they settled in for the night. They put the Awakener in the middle of the small open space and made their own beds on opposite sides of him. A thick stand of trees barred one side, and Sealeaf bedded down on the trailside. "That way," Robbie said, "if he wakes up and tries to wander away, he'll stumble into one of us, or at least with all the dried plants we should hear him."

Stefani took the first watch. Ranya sat with her for a while before yawning wide. "Your watch is over when that cluster of stars reaches the tip of that tall razor pine." The Lightwing pointed to where a dark shadowy point reached into the sky.

"Okay."

"But wake me if you hear or see anything," Ranya told her.

Stefani shivered in the chill night air and pulled her jacket tight. "Will do."

Ranya flitted over to the side-pocket of Stefani's backpack. To make it a little cozier, she'd stuffed the pocket with dried plants and tufts of animal fur she'd gathered from thorny bushes they'd passed along the way. Now, she ducked inside and lowered the pocket flap, leaving Stefani to watch the stars drift overhead.

CHAPTER THIRTY-TWO

Stefani jerked awake with a start. A heaviness had settled over her and she'd begun to nod off. She tried to rub the sleep from her eyes, but couldn't raise her arm. She struggled. Something had wrapped around her wrist and held her tight. Was she still asleep and dreaming? "Oh!" she gasped. By the faint light of the stars, she could see the outline of vines wrapped around her arms and legs. "Tanglevines! Not again."

"Mmmmph?" A muffled sound came from beside her.

"Robbie?" Stefani called out. "Sealeaf!"

"What's—" A thrashing sound came from where Robbie had been sleeping. "Are you kidding me?"

"I'm so sorry," Stefani said. "I . . . I must have dozed off for a second." She glanced up, searching the sky for the cluster of stars Ranya had pointed out to her. The unfamiliar night sky stared back at her.

Sounds of vines whispering against themselves came from the darkness.

"Don't move. They tighten if you move. Remember?" Robbie said grumpily.

"It's not me."

"Sealeaf?"

There was no response, only the sound of something thrashing around in the dried leaves. The noise stopped suddenly, replaced by a low humming.

"What's that?" Stefani whispered.

"I don't know. It sounds like . . . Oh, no. The Awakener." Robbie's voice was tinged with panic.

"What about him?" Stefani tried not to move or breathe too deeply, for fear it would cause the vines to tighten.

"He's makes things grow. What if—?" There was real fear in Robbie's voice. "What if it's him? What if he caused the vines to attack us?"

"Come on, Robbie! Give it a rest. He's not evil."

"I never said he was evil. But what if he's making them grow by accident? It's obvious he has no clue what he's doing most of the time."

Stefani considered it. "Sir?" she called out in her most respectful voice. "Could you please stop whatever it is you're doing? I mean, if you're doing anything that—"

"Just make it stop, okay?" Robbie said, through gritted teeth. "It's getting hard to breathe."

The humming grew louder.

"He's not listening," Robbie said. "Big . . . surprise."

"Ranya?" Stefani called out.

The only response was a muffled yelp from inside her back-pack pocket. The vines had climbed all over it.

"Ranya's trapped, too." Stefani said. Panic dried her mouth, causing her voice to rasp. "Sir? Please make it stop before they crush her."

The singing grew louder and, in the darkness, something moved toward her, shuffling through the dried leaves and plants. The Awakener, walking across the clearing. A dark shadow against the star-filled sky, he loomed over her, still humming. His tuneless song changed into something different as he stood beside her. It fell into the rhythm of a lullaby.

Stefani tried not to cringe, but she couldn't help herself, as wriggling Tanglevines slithered against her. But instead of gripping her tighter, they began to loosen. One by one, they dropped away, retreating back into the stand of trees beside the clearing.

"Hey!" called Robbie. "He's doing it. They're letting go." His voice was filled with relief.

Stefani leaped up, scrambling over to where she'd left her pack and opened the flap of the pocket. "Ranya. Are you okay?"

The Lightwing struggled to raise herself out of the pocket. "My wing. It's crushed." Her words gasped out through gritted teeth. "And my face feels like I just lost a sparring match with my bruiser of a cousin."

The Awakener continued to sing as woody vines dragged themselves away and out of the clearing. The silence that set in once the vines finished pulling away was unnerving. Stefani tensed, waiting for their sudden return. "Shouldn't we move on?" she finally asked.

"I'm sorry, but I don't know if I can travel, yet." Ranya grunted. "I'm not sure I can even get out of here."

"Here, let me help you." Stefani gently lifted Ranya out of the pocket.

The Lightwing hissed in pain as Stefani set her down beside her. Starlight glinted off her crushed wing.

"I'm so sorry, Ranya. I didn't mean to—"

"Not your fault." Ranya told her.

"But it was," Stefani said. "It is. All of it."

"Done is done," Ranya told her. "It's as much my fault

as yours. I should have taken first watch. I saw how tired you were."

"But—"

"Worrying at it will not fix things," Ranya told her.

Across from them the Awakener let out a loud snort. The old man had already curled up and gone back to sleep. The others spent the rest of the night wide awake. No one was able to sleep. No one, except the Awakener. He snored loudly from his place in the middle of the clearing. They huddled as far from the line of trees and the tanglevines as possible.

When the growing sunlight finally brought color back to the land, they reassessed their injuries. "That looks painful," Stefani said as she examined Ranya's wing.

Ranya glanced over her shoulder. "It's bad, but not as bad as it looks. Not permanently damaged. Only, I won't be able to fly until it's healed. So, I won't be much use to you as a scout, I'm afraid."

I will scout and lead until you heal, Sealeaf signed.

Thank you, Ranya signed back.

"Is there anything we can do?" Stefani dug through the first-aid kit, but everything was too big or too heavy for a fairy wing.

"Spider silk," Ranya said.

"Hey, what about him now that he's awake?" Robbie pointed his thumb at the Awakener, who sat up and stretched, his mouth open in a huge yawn.

Ranya shrugged, then winced. "We can at least ask."

Stefani held out her hand for Ranya to step onto and carried her over to where the Awakener sat cross-legged on the ground. He dragged his hands through the dried plants, picking up handfuls and holding them in front of him, then letting them fall. He grinned at her through the falling leaves and grasses.

Stefani knelt down in front of him and held Ranya up on the palm of her hand. "Mr. Awakener, we were wondering if you could do something to help our friend."

He tilted his head, examining the Lightwing's wounded wing, then shrugged. He reached beneath the pile of plant matter that surrounded him, and held up a tiny mushroom.

"What's that?" Stefani asked. "Will it fix your wing?"

"It won't heal me," Ranya said, a low sigh escaping her as she reached out for the fungus. "But it will help with the pain."

CHAPTER THIRTY-THREE

It took another day and a half to get back to Aurien's glen. When they arrived, exhausted and thirsty, the sun already slanted downward in the pale evening sky. Laurel's frozen silhouette against the last rays of light caused a catch in Stefani's throat. Would the Awakener be able to save her? She took his hand in hers and led him forward, hope and fear churning inside her.

Ranya rode on Robbie's pack, her damaged wing, though healing, keeping her from flight. Exhausted, Sealeaf moved like someone in a dream. Her insistence on doing most of the scouting and guarding had taken its toll.

As they trudged forward, Stefani wondered why the Awakener could make anything grow, but was unable to heal the mildest of injuries. She rubbed at her wrist where the tanglevine's grip had left her skin raw. "I guess it's just plant magic." She stopped walking. "Wait. If his magic only works on plants, how will it help Laurel? She's only part tree, right?"

Robbie barely slowed. "Like you said before, if Aurien thinks it will work, then who are we to question it?" The bitterness from before had drained out of him. Now, he just sounded tired.

Stefani looked across the field, then back at the Awakener. "Right. I guess so."

Aurien waited for them beside the little bridge that arched over the trickling stream. He looked bone-thin now and his fine white coat was tinged with gray. "Welcome back. It appears you were successful in your quest." He lowered his horn in respect.

The Awakener clapped his hands together in joy at the sight of the unicorn. "Sugar plums wear them best!"

"Pardon?" Aurien tilted his head in confusion.

"He's been like this the whole time," Robbie grumbled.

"Not the whole time," Stefani corrected. "He had some moments when he made sense. Or seemed to."

Aurien turned his head to gaze out of one eye at the old man. "This is an aspect I am unfamiliar with."

"That figures." Robbie reached a hand back and Ranya stepped onto his palm. He gently set her on the bridge railing, before slipping his empty backpack off his shoulders and dropping it on the ground. "Too bad it's not one that I'm unfamiliar with."

Stefani took off her pack as well, then tried to lead the Awakener across the little bridge. They were half way across when he stopped and refused to move another step. He leaned over the railing and stared down into the tiny rivulet. "Busy bees! Busy bees!" he shouted.

Robbie shook his head.

Stefani tried once more to guide him forward. She talked to him quietly, urging him to cross the bridge and help

Laurel. "I don't know how much time she has," she told the old man. "Please, just help her."

"Bluebird beans!" He gripped the railing and held on tight.

She tried pushing and pulling, but finally threw her hands into the air. "I don't know what to do."

"Let me try." Robbie stepped onto the bridge.

Stefani eyed him with doubt. "But you don't even like him."

He shook his head. "It's not that I don't like him, Stef." He mashed his lips together for a moment before starting again. "It's just that . . . I don't want him to be like this. Okay? I don't want him to forget who he was . . . his family . . . friends." He squeezed his eyes shut. Then he looked at the Awakener and sighed. "Only, I get now that it isn't his fault. It's just the way he is."

She nodded and wiped at her face with her bandanna. "I know."

Robbie stood beside the Awakener and put a hand on his arm. "Do you remember," he said, "the way the rain watered everything and gave it life?"

The Awakener stopped shouting nonsense words at the water and stared at Robbie. "Life?"

"Yes." Robbie took the old man by the wrists, turned him, then walked backward across the bridge. He kept talking, guiding the Awakener to the place where Laurel stood rooted to the earth. "The rain poured down and, with it, you made the forest blossom. You brought life." He stepped aside and gestured to the Treemage. "Life, Awakener. Laurel needs life. Can you give it to her?"

The Awakener stepped closer and frowned. "Life," he said, "is for the living."

Stefani felt her heart catch. "But she is alive!" She ran across the bridge and stood before Laurel, looking for some sign that the sorceress was still there, still not fully tree. But as she peered into the Treemage's face, her heart fell. There was no sign at all that Laurel still existed within the thick skin of bark that covered her from head to foot. It was nearly impossible now to make out her features, the curve of her cheekbones. Not even the small breeze that swirled through the meadow seemed to disturb the wilted leaves that remained attached to Laurel's head and trailed down her back. Stefani sagged before her friend. "We came too late," she said, fresh tears streaking her face. "We took too long. I should have listened. I should have come sooner."

"Alive," the old man said, "but no longer awake. Deep sleep. Too deep."

Aurien stepped closer and peered at the Treemage. "I'm afraid he is correct."

"But he's the Awakener. He should wake her up. That's

his job!" Stefani accused.

The Awakener looked up at the mention of his name. "Ah, yes. I see. I see." Smiling, he walked over to where Laurel stood, branches stretched skyward. He leaned down and picked up a small branch that had fallen from Laurel's hair. A single dried leaf clung stubbornly to one end. "She wishes you to have this." He held it out to Stefani, but she refused to take it.

"No." she cried. "It isn't right."

"I'm sorry," Aurien told her. "I truly am."

The Awakener nudged her with the branch. "She wants to be with you."

Stefani grabbed the stick and flung it away. "This isn't Laurel!"

Her wing still not yet mended, Ranya flitted awkwardly over the ground to where the skinny branch lay. Grasping it in the middle, the Lightwing heaved it up like a weight lifter and flew in jouncing fits over to where Robbie stood. "I know most of it seems like nonsense, but I have learned to listen to what my elders say." She panted as she tried to stay aloft, then fluttering to closer to the ground. "And they have always respected our land's caretakers, those like the Treemage." The extra weight and her twisted wing pulled her down into a rough landing. "And those like the Awakener."

Robbie took the branch from Ranya. He gazed at Stefani and tucked the sad-looking stick into his pack.

Stefani turned away, wiping at her eyes.

"I guess it can't hurt to keep it," Robbie said. "Maybe, she'll want it later."

CHAPTER THIRTY-FOUR

"What's the point?" Stefani asked, her voice sounding empty and hollow. Her eyes were still red and puffy.

"You heard Aurien," Robbie said, trying to sound hopeful. "Maybe the Awakener can fix what's wrong with Anoria, if we take him to the King."

Stefani snorted. "Sure. Like he woke up Laurel. Oh, wait. He didn't. Why don't we just leave him here?" She pulled up a handful of faded grass. "I have a better idea." She lunged forward and grabbed Robbie's hand, but nothing happened.

Robbie gently pulled his hand from hers. "You'll be glad later that didn't work."

"Whatever. I still think we should leave him here."

Sealeaf signed her disagreement, her mouth set in a

hard line and her gestures firm.

"Aurien is wise." Ranya nodded. "We must listen to wisdom."

"He's probably just trying to get us to take him off his . . ." Stefani glanced across the way to where Aurien stood talking with the old man. Standing beside one another like that, the two beings looked sort of alike. Aurien's white coat and faded hooves and horn beside the Awakener's long, white beard. It was as if they had both stepped out of some fantasy artist's idea of a unicorn and a sage. She snorted again and looked away.

Robbie scratched at the back of his neck. "I'm with Sealeaf and Ranya. We came here to help. And maybe there's still some good that can come from us being here." He brushed the palm of his hand across the stiff blades of grass beside him. "I think if there's any chance at all of helping Anoria, we need to take it. Besides, we need him along to grow supplies. He held up his pack and waved it in front of her. "I've got nothing left."

"Good luck with that. His food growing hasn't been so great."

"Then, we'll just have to make do with what we can find."

"Fine. I get it. I'm outvoted." Stefani grabbed her equally empty pack and yanked it onto her shoulders. "Emrys is the only one who can send us home, anyway. So we have to get there, in order to get back." She jabbed a finger in the direction of the Awakener. "But like you said before, he's just going to slow us down."

The old man grinned and pointed back at her, as if it was a game.

She stood up. "But I'm not going to watch him, anymore. From now on, he's your problem."

"Yeah," Robbie said, unhappy with the way things were going. He stood up and pulled on his own pack. "That figures."

CHAPTER THIRTY-FIVE

Stefani plodded along, dragging her feet in the dust. Two more days had passed and not much had changed. The Awakener still grew things, but most of what they *could* eat, tasted horrible, at least to Stefani. That morning, however, he'd caused a fruit tree to blossom and grow yellow apple-like fruit. It wasn't as sweet as the apples back home, and tasted a little like carrots. But they'd stuffed themselves and filled their packs.

Stefani still felt helpless, though. Bad enough that she had been the cause of so much terrible trouble in Anoria, but coming back here hadn't changed a thing. At least, not for Laurel. She sighed, tears pushing against the backs of her eyes. At least they'd be heading home soon. Just as soon as they delivered the Awakener to King Emrys at

Dragon's Tor.

She stumbled forward deep in thought. A cold shadow fell over her, followed by a huge familiar form that landed awkwardly on the path ahead.

She gasped and stepped back. "Greenback!"

Robbie tugged the Awakener to a stop as Sealeaf tried to duck into the greenery beside the trail. "Ah, ah, ah," the dragon said. "Stay where I can see you."

Sealeaf frowned. She stepped back onto the path beside Robbie and twitched her hands, *What do we do?*

Stefani bit her lip, her mouth dry from more than thirst. Ranya peeked out from the backpack pocket where she had been resting. Stefani shook her head, hoping Ranya would stay put. Pretending to grip her backpack straps in a nervous way, she signed back to Sealeaf, *Danger. Careful.*

"It's about time." The dragon limped forward a few paces and turned his hulking head at an odd angle. Stefani stared at the thick scar that ran down the left side of his face. "Like it?" he asked. "A gift from my previous employer, Ashkell. You might recall we had a bit of a disagreement beneath his so-called Palace." The broken dragon peered at them out of his one good eye, and Stefani shivered, remembering their close call that day. The way Ashkell had emerged from the tunnel, enraged, blood dripping from his claws.

"How? We saw the castle collapse on you." Stefani's whisper barely carried across the path to her companions, but it was clear Greenback's hearing was still as good as ever.

He curled his lip at her words. "Ah, the stinking dungeon's escape tunnel. It did get . . . cramped after the earthquake." He ran the back of his foreclaw down the scarring on his left side. "Ashkell was always brutal. Ending up where he did, tucked forever inside his precious land is an oddly fitting end. Don't you agree?"

Stefani shivered, recalling her own near plunge into the crevasse that had slammed shut over Ashkell. He'd been trapped with the Greatstone he had sought so hard to control.

Greenback leered at them. "A neat job you did of murdering him for me. Saved me from having to kill him myself." He pointed a dark claw at Stefani. "You've a fine talent for violence."

She froze, her head tingling with the memory, and guilt pricked her.

"Don't listen to him, Stef," Robbie said in a soft voice. "It was self-defense. Besides, no one made him fly into that hole after the Greatstone."

Stefani said nothing. Greenback's words still tumbled though her brain. *Murder. Kill. Talent for violence.*

"With such a bent for killing, it must be a great surprise to see you did not succeed in eliminating me, as well." He adjusted his weight awkwardly. "You forget. I have always survived by being more clever than others. Even your tree witch." He grinned wickedly with the side of his mouth that still worked, showing a broken fang. "I had planned for nearly every possibility. Although, the trapping of the Greatstone was an unexpected twist." He stroked his sagging chin with a foreclaw. "But even that, I was able to turn to my own purpose in the end."

Greenback's half-grin made him look even more frightening. "I guess after all of that you weren't expecting *me*," he said. "But I've been expecting *you*. I knew you'd be unable to resist a call from that 'meddling witch." He lurched forward, limping closer to them.

"You sent the message?" Stefani took another small step back.

"Oh, no. Not I." Greenback let go a wheezing cough. "But I knew you'd hear her, once I pulled her into the worldspell and encouraged the path of her dreams." He raised a shoulder and let it drop, as if half a shrug was all he could manage. "A few of the more important books survived the toppling of Ashkell's domain. And I was not in a position to travel after the havoc you two wreaked on my plans." His foreclaws balled into fists and he coughed again, his whole body shaking with it.

"He's weak," Robbie said, under his breath.

"Someone didn't grow," the Awakener blurted.

"What did you say, old man?" Greenback raised his eye to stare at the Awakener.

"Shhhh." Robbie patted the old man's arm. "Ignore him," he told Greenback. "He doesn't know what he's saying."

"Don't tell me what to do, boy!" Greenback lunged forward, jaw snapping shut inches from Robbie and the Awakener.

"My, what big teeth," the old man reached a hand toward Greenback's broken incisor.

The dragon started and stumbled back, nearly tripping

over his own tail before regaining his balance. "You'll pay for that!"

Ranya took the opportunity to quietly leap from her hiding place and up into the branches of a nearby tree, making a quiet but awkward landing.

"In for a penny, in for a peony." The Awakener chuckled. He held out a fresh bloom, offering it to the angry dragon.

Fuming, Greenback shifted his weight, extended his vicious claws, prepared to leap at the old man.

"Wait!" Stefani shouted. "We don't want trouble. Just tell us what you want."

Her shout caught Greenback by surprise. He stared at her for a moment. And then he began to laugh.

"What's so funny?" Robbie asked.

This struck the dragon as even funnier. A small chuckle at first, Greenback's laughter grew until Stefani cringed. Robbie held his hands over his ears.

Soon he was doubled over, wheezing and coughing.

Sealeaf glanced at Robbie, who waved his fingers at her in a motion for retreat.

But as soon as she took a step back, Greenback's laughter ceased. "Stop!" He stood panting, but he was clearly prepared to pounce.

Everyone froze.

"I have what I want. My plan is nearly complete. The so-called leaders of this land are dying, fading away. Their offspring remain frozen, unable to hatch. Your precious Treemage is trapped within her own element. And, as for Emrys, well, he has finally learned that the connection with the land works both ways." He turned his head sharply to the left, cracking the bones in his powerful neck.

Stefani stared at his scarred face, his broken frame, the way his scales looked more faded than she remembered. "You're tied to it, too," she murmured, as the truth of how far he was willing to go for revenge struck her.

Greenback's upper lip curled. "An unfortunate side-effect of the spell. But a price I was willing to pay." He rubbed at his left side, where the pale, puckered scars from Ashkell's ripping talons stood out against his green scales. "Not that I haven't already paid the price to have what I deserve."

"Not a peony? Then, perhaps, a snapdragon?" The Awakener giggled and held out a yellow flower.

Greenback's nostrils flared. "I don't know who you are, old man. But you die first." He started forward, but the flower in the Awakener's hand suddenly grew and bloomed into a scaly plant. Long spines sprouted along its stem, sticking out in every direction. "Ahhhh!" Greenback stopped in his tracks, his eyes watering and snout quivering. "Dragon's bane? What sort of wizard are you?" His breathing was ragged and wheezy.

"He's not a wizard," Robbie said, "he's—"

"A magician!" Stefani shouted over Robbie, who turned to stare at her. She shook her head at him and his eyes grew round. "His name is, um, Magical Max," Stefani said, using the first name that came into her head, "And he's . . . he's all powerful."

Greenback narrowed his watery eyes. "I've never heard of him."

"Well, you wouldn't have," Robbie joined in. "He's from our world. And he's so powerful, he can bring someone back from being mostly dead."

"Yeah," Stefani said. "I bet he could even heal you, in spite of what you've done to the land."

Sealeaf stared at them in confusion.

"But he won't help you, if you hurt him. Or, any of us," Robbie added quickly.

Greenback's eyes narrowed. "He will help me, or I will do more than hurt you."

"You were going to do that, anyway." Stefani crossed her arms over her chest.

Greenback sneezed. "Fine. I won't hurt you. *If*, and only

if, the old skeleton can heal me. *Completely.*"

Stefani glanced at Robbie. He pursed his lips together and shrugged.

"And tell him to get rid of that horrible plant, or I'll rip you all into tiny pieces, right now." Greenback sniffed so loud, it sounded like a steam locomotive.

"Um, Sir," Stefani said, hoping the Awakener would understand. "Could you please make that go away?" She pointed at the dragon's bane.

The old man grinned and shrugged and let the spiny plant wilt and fall to the ground. Stefani and Robbie both sighed in relief.

They were all still alive. For now. Only, one big problem remained; how they were going to escape from Greenback.

Stefani sidled closer to Robbie. "We need to think fast," she said under her breath, hoping Greenback was too busy sniffling and sneezing to hear her.

"I know."

Stefani searched the forest around them for something, anything, that might help.

"Get that thing away!" Greenback shouted, holding his claws over his snout, and trying not to breathe in any of the dead plant's pollen.

Stefani kicked the remains of the plant behind them and into the trees.

Ranya saluted as she dropped down on silent wings to gather up the remains of the allergen-filled flower. Robbie nodded at them in understanding.

"Hey, Stef, do you still have that crystal I gave you?" Robbie murmured.

Stefani felt the color rising into her cheeks, recalling the small treasure she carried in her pocket. "Um, I might."

Robbie looked at her in surprise. "I thought you liked it."

"I did. I do." She hoped he couldn't see how hard she was blushing.

"Well, do you still have it or not?"

"Yes, I have it." She reached into her front pocket and pulled it out. "See."

Robbie's face brightened. He held out his hand for the glittering rock.

"What do you want with it?" Stefani dropped it into his palm.

"We need a distraction to buy someone some time." He raised an eyebrow. "And I have an idea."

CHAPTER THIRTY-SIX

"Stop that whispering and tell me how this magic works," Greenback demanded, his heavy wheezing growing louder with his frustration. "I'm not some hatchling that can be tricked into a spell."

"We know that." Robbie nodded earnestly at the menacing dragon.

The Awakener toddled forward and began walking around Greenback, ogling him.

"What's he doing?" Greenback edged away from the old man, turning in a circle to keep his eyes on him.

"Him?" Stefani tried to grab at the old man's sleeve, but he pulled away and kept circling Greenback. "He's, um, he's assessing. Checking the extent of the damage."

"Yeah," Robbie chimed in. "He has to use just the right

amount of power. Too much and..."

"And I'll grind you all into the dirt where you belong," Greenback snarled. "You meddling little mammals."

"Sticks and stones." The Awakener smiled and nodded. "Stones and sticks."

"What does that mean? What's he saying?" Greenback leaned away from the Awakener, who continued to walk around the huge dragon, wiggling his fingers at him.

"This stone came from our world and it's heavy with technological magic." Robbie used the opportunity to reveal the crystal in his hand. It glittered in the half-light.

"Techno-what?" Greenback eyed Robbie in suspicion.

"Gadget magic," Robbie ad-libbed. "Just the most powerful magic there is in our world. Watch this." He took out his phone and, holding the stone beside it, pushed the power button on. The phone screen lit up and it chimed. Good thing he'd thought to turn it off and save the battery.

"What is that?" Greenback asked, leaning forward, curiosity making him forget about the old man who stalked him like a hungry mosquito.

"It's a container for the techno-power." Robbie was warming to his subject. "I have to fill it up using this powerful crystal." He shook the stone over the phone as if he was shaking something out of it and into the cell phone.

"Now, I just need to make sure the battery is full—"

Greenback's head whipped around, his eyes filled with a mix of fear and anger. "If there is any battering to be done, it will be by me," he threatened.

"No, no," Stefani corrected. "That's not what he meant. A battery...this kind of battery...is a power cell, a place to store the, um, magical energy."

"For the healing spell," Robbie said. He glanced out of the corner of his eye, trying to find Ranya in the shadows between the trees. But there was no sign of the Lightwing.

Sealeaf signed something short while leaning her head back and to the right, as if stretching, but Robbie caught her meaning. Sealeaf was keeping a watch out for Ranya and would let them know when the time was right.

Robbie opened his phone's settings and clicked on the sounds menu.

Greenback watched him, his good eye narrowed in suspicion.

Robbie quick-scrolled to the bell chime and tapped it. The phone let out a small "ding" and Greenback jumped back nervously. "What was that?"

"That was the sound of you getting what you deserve," Robbie said, taking a quick step back.

"What?" Greenback tilted his head in confusion. Before he could make another move, Ranya dropped out of the trees and dove downward. She launched an armload of ground-up Dragon's Bane petals into his face.

Greenback roared, swatting at the Lightwing, but even with her half-healed wing, Ranya was quick. She flapped out of range as his claws raked the air where she had been. With another ferocious roar, Greenback began to paw at his face. "My eye!" He stumbled back and forth, attempting to clear his vision, but his eye was swelling shut and he began to sneeze, one fierce blast after another.

"Run!" Stefani yelled, yanking the Awakener's sleeve and dodging away from the flailing dragon.

Sealeaf and Robbie headed for the forest, but the Awakener yanked out of Stefani's grip and stood his ground. He watched Greenback with an odd look on his face.

Stefani spun around and sped back to the old man, gripping his hand. "Come on! We need to go!"

But the Awakener shook his head. "The season has passed."

"You're doomed," Greenback shouted, shuffling in a circle, trying to focus his bleary eye. His wicked talons extended, he ripped at the air.

"Robbie, help me!" Stefani shouted. She pulled at the Awakener, but he stood rooted in place.

Robbie and Sealeaf rushed back to help, Ranya flitting above them.

Greenback's vision landed on the Awakener and he lurched toward him.

"No!" Stefani shouted, tugging at the old man's arm, but it was too late.

Greenback raked his wicked talons across the Awakener's chest at the same time as the old man reached out and placed a hand on Greenback's forearm. Light erupted around them with a crack like thunder.

Greenback screamed and rose into the sky. A bright green aura surrounded him.

Robbie shielded his eyes as a sudden burst of light and color filled the air.

When the light faded, Robbie blinked against the brightness that swirled in his vision. Finally, his eyesight cleared and he heard Stefani gasp in shock.

The Awakener lay in a ragged heap on the ground.

There was no sign of Greenback.

CRRO
RORR

CHAPTER THIRTY-SEVEN

Stefani sat on the ground, tears falling freely down her face. She didn't even try to wipe them away.

There was still no sign of Greenback. The Awakener lay on the ground, staring up at the blue sky and the scudding clouds. He beckoned her close, his lips moving, but his words too low for her to hear.

Stefani leaned nearer.

"Give it to me," the old man said, holding out his wrinkled hand.

"What?" Stefani asked in confusion.

"Laurel's offering," he said between panted breaths. "Give...it to...me."

Robbie unzipped his pack, pulled out the branch he'd picked up, and offered it to her with shaking hands "Here."

"Thanks." She choked back a sob as she held it out to the Awakener.

The Awakener held the branch for only a moment. Then, he handed it back to Stefani and touched her cheek with the backs of his fingers.

His words faltered, turning into low murmurs. "Twig and leaf...beating heart...sleeping spirit...touch of magic." His hand slowly slipped away from her face.

Stefani reached out to twine the fingers of one hand in his. "What?" she asked. "I don't understand."

"Restore the heart...of Anoria." He smiled. His hand relaxed, fingers slipping from hers. Then his eyes fluttered closed.

"No!" Stefani cried out. "I don't know what that means. And...and I'm sorry! I didn't mean any of the things I said." Tears rolled down her face. She dropped the branch and gripped a handful of the Awakener's robe, trying to shake him awake. "Please, don't go..." She looked off into the distance, where Dragon's Tor loomed over the forest. "Look. We're almost there."

He lay still, no longer breathing. Around them grass sprouted. Flowers blossomed. Vines twined. Plants grew up and over the Awakener, forming a lush bower above him.

Stefani stood up and backed away. The greenery thickened around the Awakener until she could no longer see him. Tears streamed down her face. Her chest tightened. She wanted to curl into a ball and stay there.

Robbie put a hand on her shoulder. "It's okay, Stef. I think he knew, in his own way." His voice was thick with emotion.

Stefani shook her head. Their quest was filled with pain and suffering, failure and death. She reached down and picked up Laurel's branch and cradled it in her hands. "First Laurel, and now the Awakener," she said, trying to keep from sobbing. "Why did we even come here?"

Sealeaf crept closer to the greenery that had grown over

the old man and placed her beaded necklace on a small leafy branch. She signed her sorrow and goodbye over it and backed away, her head bowed.

Ranya, wings drooping, fluttered back to Robbie's shoulder, then let out a startled, "Oh."

Robbie reached for his pocketknife. "What is it?"

"It's growing." Ranya pointed to the stick in Stefani's hand.

"What?" Stefani sniffed and glanced down, then held up the tiny branch. A green shoot with tiny silver buds had sprouted on it.

"Is that...?" Robbie gazed at the new growth.

"It's...it's Laurel's branch," Stefani said in amazement. "It's budding." Her fingers shook as she held the branch out where they all could see.

Life! Sealeaf signed in excitement.

"Yes," Ranya said. "It's come back to life."

"Twig and leaf," Stefani said in a quiet voice.

"What?" Robbie's brows wrinkled in confusion.

"It's what the Awakener said, part of his last words to me." Stefani's voice caught as she repeated the words, "Twig and leaf. Restore the heart." She gripped the branch in her hands. "I know what we have to do."

CHAPTER THIRTY-EIGHT

They walked through the forest for hours. When they finally stepped out from under the dying branches, the world hadn't crashed to an end, but Stefani felt like a shirt that had been ripped apart at the seams. How could she really know from his confused words what the Awakener had wanted her to do? How could she be sure that his final words weren't just more crazy thoughts that had popped into his mixed-up brain?

And why should any of it matter now? Laurel was forever asleep in Aurien's Glen, and the Awakener . . .

And where was Greenback? Was he somewhere ahead, lying in wait for them? She tried not to think about all the awful ways he should be punished. Tried not to wish horrid things on him. But this was his fault. All of it.

Not all of it, she reminded herself. Some of the blame belonged to her.

"I know what you're thinking." Robbie stepped up beside her and matched her pace.

She kept walking, unable to bring herself to argue with him.

"It's not your fault, Stef. Not our fault. It was Greenback. All of this . . . " he waved his arm at the dead and dying world around them. "This is his fault. And what happened with the Awakener . . ." his voice cracked and dropped to a whisper. "He was really brave."

His face crumpled with sadness. It brought her out of her own dark place. She wanted to take his hand, to comfort him. "I'm sorry about the Awakener." Her words were thick in her throat. "I'm sorry about Laurel." She took a deep breath, then plowed on. "And I am so sorry about your grandfather."

Robbie nodded. "Me, too. All of it. And I hate how much of a jerk I've been. Especially, about Gramps."

"You're not a jerk, Robbie."

"Yeah," he said, "I am. At least, I've totally been acting like one. Gramps was—is an amazing man. He fought in the war, you know. He even got a medal. After that, he worked for civil rights. Then, when he retired, he did volunteer stuff." He turned his head away for a moment and when he turned back his eyes glistened. "He is one of the smartest, bravest people I know. I just hate feeling like I'm losing him when he's still right in front of me. I know it's not his fault, but I've been so angry. And I've been taking it out on him."

They walked in silence for a while before he cleared his throat and wiped his face on his sleeve. "It's just the way it is, I suppose. There's nothing anyone can do about it."

"Well, we can't fix those things," Stefani said, "but maybe, just maybe, we can do something about the damage Greenback did here." She reached back and patted her backpack where the tiny branch held bright green buds.

"Maybe we can do what Laurel wanted us to. Maybe we can save Anoria."

CHAPTER THIRTY-NINE

They were ragged and tired when they finally reached Dragon's Tor, but instead of resting, they had insisted on seeing the king.

It had taken time for them to convince the king to let them test Stefani's idea. He'd remained unmoved until they had told him everything: Laurel and the dreams, Greenback's attack on the land, and the Awakener's final words. Finally, Stefani showed him the budding branch. "The Heart of Anoria is a place dear to us," he said.

"Is it near by?" Robbie asked.

Emris frowned. "Yes, but it is currently occupied. . . by my Queen. And she is not accepting visitors."

"But this could save Anoria," Stefani insisted. "Don't you think she'll want to let us try?"

"I will take you to the Queen's chamber, but I cannot guarantee she will allow us in. She has not been herself these past weeks. Each day she grows angrier, more detached," Emrys told them in a rush. His words showed his discouragement, but his excited actions seemed fueled by a fearful hope.

He led them through the cavernous palace. Wide hallways were cut deep into the glittering stone, the floors polished smooth from the passage of dragons over the centuries. Where torchlight fell onto the floor, it shone like a dark mirror.

One after another, they passed broad passageways that crisscrossed the main passage and branched off deeper into the mountain.

Sealeaf stared at everything, as if she wanted to capture it all. Ranya sat on her friend's shoulder, taking it all in, as well.

"Whoa. This place is huge," Robbie said as they followed the king deeper and deeper into the heart of the mountain. "It seems so much bigger inside than I thought."

Stefani nudged him with an elbow. "You have a beautiful home," she said.

The king kept walking, but he turned his head and looked at them out of one eye. "It would be more beautiful with the scampering of hatchlings echoing through these corridors," he sighed. "The gaiety of offspring would shine brighter than the richest crystal veins within our home." His voice was filled with sadness.

Finally, they stood before a great wood and metal doorway. The thick doors that barred their way were deeply carved with the images of a pair of magnificent dragons circling one another in flight. The heavy hinges and doorknobs were darkened with age. Emrys raised his huge foreclaw and tapped lightly on the door with a single talon.

"Go away!" an angry voice roared.

"Sylmara," Emrys called gently. "It's only me."

"Do not lie to me. You are not alone," hissed the voice. "Who have you brought now to see me in my sorrow? Another of your worthless advisors, perhaps? Another inept midwife?"

Emrys turned to face them. "I apologize," he told them. "As I told you, Sylmara is not herself. Please wait here while I go in and speak with her."

He turned back to the door. "Sylmara, I need you to let me in. Please, Fire of my Heart."

On the other side of the door, a heavy bar slammed into the wall. Emrys took a deep breath, then he pulled gently on the ornate handles, and the massive doors opened outward without a sound.

The king stepped inside and the doors swung shut, leaving the weary travelers standing in the cavernous hallway.

The king and queen spoke low, their voices muffled behind the great doors.

"I hope this works," Robbie said as Stefani took out the small twig the Awakener had given her and turned it over in her hands. Suddenly, she thrust it at him. "You do it. I just...I can't."

"I'm sorry, Stef." He examined the tiny buds that peeked out along the edges. "But are you sure about this?"

She nodded, wiping her damp eyes with her ragged bandanna.

Ranya shifted on Sealeaf's shoulder. "There's life in it. So much, it nearly pulses with it."

"Really?" Robbie peered closer, but other than the tiny buds, he didn't sense anything unusual. "It just seems like there should be more to it than this."

Hope, Sealeaf signed.

"Yes." Stefani shoved the bandanna into her pocket. "We have to hope it works." She twisted the silver band on her finger. "King Emrys looks so sad and...worn. He's wasting away, just like the land of Anoria."

"It's the connection," Robbie said. "Like Greenback said, the land is tied to Emrys. I guess that means that Emrys is tied to the land, too."

"And Laurel is too, now." Stefani shook her head. "It's just so . . . awful."

"I guess that's why the Awakener couldn't wake her up," Robbie said, "and why he . . ."

"I'm sorry," Stefani said. "I really am. I don't know why I was so mean to him."

"*You* were mean to him? I was a total jerk." He stared at his feet.

"I get it." Stefani stroked the budding branch with a fingertip. "You were upset about more than him."

They were quiet for a while lost in their own thoughts.

"It's all right." Robbie finally broke the silence. "I think he knew you didn't mean any of it. You were just upset about Laurel."

Stefani bit her lip. "That doesn't make it okay. The last thing I said to him before—"

"Don't make yourself feel extra bad over it." Robbie's voice caught. "He probably didn't even remember."

The massive doors swung open and King Emrys beckoned to them with a foreclaw. "Queen Sylmara, Breath of the Sun, Winged Star of the Night, will see you now." He shook his head wearily. "But only Robbie and Stefani."

"But I am their guide," Ranya complained, averting her eyes at the angry snort of smoke that erupted from the king's nostrils.

Sealeaf bowed low, then signed that she should be included, as well.

The king looked thoughtful, then glanced back over his shoulder. "The risk . . ."

"We've come all this way as a team," Stefani told him.

"We wouldn't be here if we hadn't stuck together," Robbie agreed.

King Emrys shook his head. "All right, I haven't the

energy to argue, but please keep in mind that my queen is . . . not herself."

"We understand," Stefani said.

"And we'll be respectful," Robbie added.

Sealeaf and Ranya both nodded.

Emrys moved aside to allow them to pass.

They stepped through the doorway, peering into the dim room.

Before them the Queen shifted and writhed, her great head swinging back and forth on her long neck as she eyed them in suspicion. Her scales shimmered a ghostly shade of pale against the shadows of the room. Before her, upon a bed of sand, sat at least a dozen large eggs, each one as big as Robbie and Stefani. The shells of the eggs were covered in fine scales and the sand radiated warmth, as if they sat atop a giant heater.

Robbie's face felt warm; his forehead grew damp with perspiration.

"It's the heart of the mountain," Emrys told them. "The earth fires still burn deep below us. Not as hot as once they did, but enough to..."

The queen let out an angry snort.

"This nursery," he continued, "along with several other clutch beds, lie here at the lowest levels of our mountain home. Where the earth's heat can keep the...eggs warm, help them develop."

Robbie stared at the huge eggs, imagining the dragon babies incubating inside them. He took a step forward, the tiny branch in his outstretched hand.

Queen Sylmara lunged without warning. Scales flashed as she spread her wings wide, wrapping them about the clutch of eggs. She thrust her head forward like a snake striking, stopping just inches from Robbie's face.

"Robbie, watch out!" Stefani shouted.

Sylmara hissed and his gaze flicked to her. She narrowed her eyes in warning. "Stay back. All of you," the Queen commanded.

Sealeaf crouched as if ready for a fight and Ranya's hand went to her sword hilt, but Emrys gave them a sharp look and shook his head. "Hold," he commanded.

Sealeaf and Ranya bowed their heads in obedience to the high king, but their eyes flickered between the queen and Robbie.

Queen Sylmara turned one angry eye on Stefani, but kept her maw directly in front of Robbie. "What do you think you are doing, mammal?" She spoke low and slow.

Robbie froze, one foot still poised to step onto the sand of the dragon's nest. His pulse raced and sweat trickled down the side of his face.

The queen inhaled deeply. "Man-child. I can hear your heartbeat." A wicked smile spread across her face.

"Sylmara," Emrys whispered, his body tense. "No."

"No?" she hissed, rearing back. "No? What if the ancient blood magic can save our children? What if the balance owed is life?"

Robbie stared up into the Queen's huge face. Her nostrils were the size of hubcaps, her teeth like a row of sharpened fence posts. He held out the small branch. All that remained of the Treemage. All that was left of Laurel Silverbark, and the last remaining buds of the Awakener's gift. "The Awakener gave us this," he told her, his voice shaking despite his effort to stay calm. "He said . . . we think. . ." He flicked his eyes to Stefani and then back to the Queen. "I didn't understand before. I couldn't see it." He licked his lips. "These..." He nodded toward the eggs. "Your children. They are the heart of Anoria."

"You dare come at my children with a stick?" The Queen reared back her mighty head to strike.

Before she could connect with her target, Emrys leaped between her and Robbie. The queen drove around him, her great teeth gleaming. Her jaws snapped just short of Robbie's head, her hot breath stinging his face, as the king struggled to hold her back.

Robbie stumbled away and Sealeaf stepped forward to help him keep his balance. Ranya hovered beside him, nervous fingers wrapping and unwrapping around the hilt of her sword.

Stefani squared her shoulders and strode forward. "It's not just a stick," she shouted, her voice thick. "It's...it's a part of Anoria. Robbie's right. Your offspring are the heart of the land, here at the root of the earth." She wiped her face with the back of her hand. "This branch represents the sun and sky. It represents...life."

"Sylmara," Emrys said, "we have nothing to lose in the attempt."

The Queen stopped straining against her mate and glared at Robbie and Stefani. "If you harm my brood, your lives are forfeit," she hissed. "Not even a king's strength will be enough to hold back my wrath." She snapped at the king, pushing away from him.

Emrys tried to soothe her, but she jerked away, scales bristling with anger.

Stefani nodded at Robbie.

One careful step at a time, he made his way across the hot sand into the middle of the nest. Once at the center, he knelt down and scooped out a small hole in the sand and leaned forward to place the small branch into it.

"Wait!" Stefani called out.

"What now?" the queen roared, pushing against Emrys once more.

Robbie froze, his hand holding the stick above the small hole he'd made. "What's up?" he asked. "I thought..."

Stefani hesitated.

"It's kind of hot over here," he said between gritted teeth. He shifted his weight onto one knee and then the other.

Queen Sylmara hissed in frustration. "Why do you delay? What trick are you playing at?"

"I think we need something more." Stefani twisted the silver band until it came off her finger and held it up for Queen Sylmara to see. Then she tiptoed across the scorching sand and placed it into the hole.

Robbie stared at her. "Are you sure?"

Stefani nodded. "A touch of magic," she said, already missing the little band of silver and hoping she was right, that they were doing the right thing. "He said 'sleeping spirit'..." She pointed to the branch. "And 'touch of magic.'"

Robbie placed the small stem into the hole. Working together, they scooped the black sand up around the branch until it could stand without help. They backed away, careful to avoid touching any of the eggs as they stepped out of the nest.

Stefani wiped her hands on her jeans.

They stood, watching and waiting for something to happen.

The small twig stuck up out of the sand, a sad thin bit of wood. The only sign of life were the teensy buds that had not grown since the Awakener had last touched it.

Sylmara leaned forward, eyeing the stick, desperation and hope warring in her face. Finally, she let out a pained groan and sank down onto her belly, her scales falling limp. "My children," she cried, tears forming in her golden eyes. "My children are doomed." Her tears hissed and spattered as they fell onto the hot sand.

***

"I'm so sorry," Stefani said, her own eyes misting up. "We thought I had the answer. Helping the Queen—"

"Look," Robbie said. All eyes turned toward him. "Not at me." He stared at the center of the nest. "There." He pointed in the direction of the stick, but it wasn't just a twig anymore. It had grown, was still growing. It pushed up from the sand, reaching higher and sprouting thin branches. Tiny silver buds dotted every branch.

Stefani gasped.

"The land is healing," Emrys murmured. "I can feel it."

Ranya danced in the shimmering air, and Sealeaf placed her palm at her chest and signed for joy.

Robbie grinned. "We did it, Stef."

The tree, for in the blink of an eye it had grown taller than Robbie, began to shiver. It spread its branches, reaching upward. Tiny crystals formed along its limbs and silver leaves sprouted from the buds. They gave off a tinkling musical sound. Finally, the tree's highest branches brushed the top of the cavern. With a shudder, the blossoming tree stopped growing up and spread it's canopy ovr the sandy bed.

It glittered in the flickering torchlight. Silver leaves moved slowly, fluttering lightly, though no breeze breathed against them. Shivering musical notes fell from the crystals onto the sand below.

"It's beautiful," Stefani whispered. Her chest ached, her heart thudding in a confused dance of joy and sorrow. It was indeed like having a bit of Laurel here, though the sorceress slept on in Aurien's Glen. At least, she's in a good place, Stefani thought.

"Yes," answered Sylmara, in breathless amazement. "Beautiful." But the golden dragon was no longer looking at the glittering tree. Her gaze was glued to something else in the nest.

"Woot!" Robbie shouted and Stefani gave him a sharp look, but Sylmara and Emrys didn't seem to notice. The expectant parents only had eyes for the pale green egg with the long threadlike crack forming across the top of it.

CHAPTER FORTY

"Oh," Stefani cried out. "This one has plum-colored eyes!" Sitting up, the baby dragon came up to her chin.

Sylmara snorted, tiny puffs of smoke rising from her nostrils as she peered down at the latest hatchling and shook her great head. "Amethyst," she corrected. "And that shall be his name."

The baby dragon stretched up toward his mother's snout and gave her a tiny nip. Sylmara grinned, showing her huge teeth. "Good greetings, Amethyst." She reached out a talon and stroked his chin. The baby dragon cooed and snuggled against his mother.

"I think this one is next." Robbie called from the other side of the nest. They turned to watch the largest of the eggs as it rocked in the warm sand. Sylmara's breath caught. "I had only hoped . . ." Her whisper echoed back from the walls of the cavern.

With a shudder, the egg rolled onto its side and cracked open. A golden snout broke through the shell, followed by the rest of the shimmering baby dragon. This one was larger than any of the others and, unlike the awkward scrabbling of its clutch-mates, shifted out of the egg in one graceful motion.

"A golden female!" Emrys shouted, his voice echoing loud in the cavern. "We have a future queen!" He stretched his neck forward and nuzzled Sylmara while admiring the newest of their brood. The newly hatched dragon stretched her wings and hopped from one foot to the other as if she would take flight then and there.

"She's impatient for the sky," Sylmara said, watching the she-dragon cavort. "Solara?"

Emrys started. "That was...my mother's name," he said quietly.

"And she was truly one with the sky. Does it displease you?" Sylmara asked, wrapping her long tail around her mate.

"No, my queen. It pleases me well," he said. "Solara is a perfect name."

A loud cracking startled them. It came from beneath the hot sand near the center of the pit.

Emrys stepped forward.

"Wait," Sylmara told him, her face filling with a new wonder.

"What is it?" Emrys asked.

"I had no reason to hope," said the Queen. "No reason to believe . . ."

Emrys eyed his queen. "Believe what?"

The cracking grew louder. The sand at the center of the pit shifted and churned.

With a spray of sand, a small green head popped into view.

"The misshapen egg?" Emrys asked, his face a mass of confused emotions. "I thought . . ."

"I couldn't bear to allow them to remove it," Sylmara whispered low. "Not with . . . I just couldn't let go of any of them." She crept across the sand, gently nudging her herd of dragonets as she moved. They chirped and squawked, opening and closing their drying wings. They followed behind her, huddling close to their mother as she approached the fresh new face. The baby dragon was still mostly buried.

Its small head swiveled in her direction, eyes swirling with recognition. Then the tiny dragon squirmed its way out of the sand and leaped toward Sylmara.

"She's whole, Emrys," she said, relief coloring her words.

"They are all whole and hatched. Every one."

Emrys beamed as Sylmara lowered herself down onto the sand where she could be closer to her hatchlings, a happy smile lighting her face. "Yes, My Fire," he said, settling in beside her. "All are whole."

Stefani grinned. "They sure look happy," she murmured to Robbie.

"Yeah." He blushed. "It's getting kind of mushy in here."

Stefani stared up at the glittering tree. "Will it be okay, do you think?"

Robbie followed her gaze. "Yeah," he said. "I think a lot of things are going to be okay."

CHAPTER FORTY-ONE

"So, you can just send us back like last time?" Stefani asked, a hint of worry in her voice.

She sat in the shade beneath a huge outcropping of rock, talking to Emrys while Robbie and the others enjoyed the last of the feast Anoria's new Awakener had caused to grow. Stefani still didn't quite understand how that all worked. She only knew that the young hatchling dragon, the tiny one that had come from the egg buried beneath the nesting sand, seemed to make things grow wherever she went. It was a joy to watch her cavort with her siblings and see the looks of surprise that came over them as flowers sprang up when she passed. Sealeaf and Ranya were both completely in awe of the dragon. Together they kept watch over her, rarely letting him out of their sight.

None of the land's inhabitants seemed the least bit surprised by it, including Aurien who had made the long journey to Dragon's Tor and arrived just in time to see the hatchlings take their first steps outside the nesting cavern. Stefani had gaped in surprise at the foliage that seem to follow the dragonet, but Aurien had merely bowed his head as the youngling passed.

Robbie had hoped to see Gamdol, but his old friend had been unable to make the long trip from the Glimmering village. Age and his responsibilities kept his old friend away, but Gamdol had sent a gift; a beautiful, hand-carved second cycle staff, complete with questing marks that represented both of Robbie's journeys in Anoria. Robbie sat beside Sealeaf, who admired the wonderful staff and gestured to him, pointing out each carving and attempting to explain their meanings.

Ranya sat on a nearby branch stuffing herself on sweet blossom nectar, wings buzzing joyfully. "Thank you again for sending the sweet blossom harvest to the Lightwings, King Emrys," she said as she licked her fingers.

"Of course," Emrys said, glowing with pride. "But you should truly thank young Verys. They seem to sprout whenever she's happiest. The oddest thing is the way they regrow their bounty as soon as they have been harvested."

He returned his attention to Stefani whose face still wore a deep worried look. "You needn't be fearful of being stranded here," he told her.

She bit her lip and reached for the silver ring, but her finger was bare. "That's not it," she said. "I just . . . I'm just not sure I'm ready to say good-bye for good."

"You won't be coming back, then?"

Stefani shrugged. "The first time, the Greatstone accidentally brought us. I mean, I don't know how it ended up in our world. And I sure didn't know what it was when I picked it up." She took a sip of her water. "And this time . . . it was Laurel. She called to me and then her ring brought us here. But now . . ." She held up her empty hand.

Emrys stared a moment before his face filled with realization. "Oh, yes. You used the ring to bring life back to the land." He bowed his head. "And our brood." He glanced behind him to where Queen Sylmara stood guard over their young. The dragonlings bounced and leaped, stretching their growing wings. "For which we can never thank you enough."

"That magic combined with Laurel's..." Stefani couldn't bring herself to finish.

"Speaking of Laurel," Aurien chimed in, "I have heard from the brownies watching over her that she has shed her dried leaves and new growth has sprouted."

"Is it possible...?" Stefani's voice filled with a desperate hope.

"Anything is possible," Aurien told her.

A huge weight lifted from Stefani and a tightness she hadn't realized had constricted her chest released, allowing her to breathe again. She glanced at Robbie in concern. "But then, if we go home and we can't get back...we'll never know." It was one of the reasons she and Robbie had agreed to stay for a while.

Emrys looked thoughtful. "I believe that both times you traveled to our realm, you arrived when you were most needed." He turned his attention to the land that stretched down from Dragon's Tor and spread into the distance, and Stefani's gaze followed his.

The sun's rays glanced off the rivers and lakes. The water reflected the light like diamonds. Here and there, the brown of the dying land had already begun to turn green again as life returned to Anoria. "I think," Emrys said quietly, "if a time comes again when you are needed, or if you truly wish to return, you will find your way back to us."

Stefani nodded, but her head still buzzed with worry. Did the King really believe that? Or was he simply trying to make her feel better? She peered into his huge eyes, and saw no doubt there. It wasn't a promise exactly, but knowing that Emrys believed it to be true made her feel less like this would be the last of their adventures in Anoria.

CRﬂ

ﬂCR

CHAPTER FORTY-TWO

Stefani's cellphone rang, playing, "You've Got a Friend in Me," the ringtone she'd set for Robbie. They'd been home for a week now, and he'd called her almost every day, but she never tired of hearing his voice. She grinned and put down her math book, then picked up the phone. "Hi Robbie. What's up?"

"Hey, Stef," Robbie said.

"Hey, what?"

"Um, are you busy?" His voice sounded uncertain.

"Nope. Just taking a much-needed break from math."

There was a long silence on the phone.

Stefani held the phone away from her face to check that the call hadn't dropped. "You still there?" she asked.

"Yeah," Robbie said, then cleared his throat. "You want

to maybe do something together on Saturday?"

"You mean something that doesn't involve deadly wasps, disgusting slime and impossible quests?"

He laughed into the phone. "Yeah. Exactly."

"Sure," Stefani said, smiling. "That'd be great. What did you have in mind?"

"Well . . . " Robbie was quiet for another long moment and Stefani held her breath, wondering what he might be planning to ask her.

"My grandfather moved into his new place. I thought maybe you'd like to go with me to visit him," he said finally.

Stefani grinned. "Absolutely," she said. "I'd like that."

"Okay, great."

On the other end of the phone, she could hear the smile in his voice.

THANK YOUS

Thank you, from the bottom of my heart, to the many fabulous readers who asked and then waited so long for this sequel. Thank you for falling in love with Robbie and Stefani, I hope you have enjoyed traveling with them again as much as I have.

A book is a collaborative effort. It springs from the heart and mind of the writer, taking root as it does, but does not reach its full potential until it has been nurtured and given the chance to grow into fullness, a process that takes many hands and hearts.

A bounty of thanks to my Beta Readers, especially Dawn V. and Linda J. for all the kind attention they have given my work over the years, helping to weed, water and trim my words, your feedback and support have once more helped my story reach wholeness.

As always, to my amazing editor, Anne Lind, who helps to tend the story and guide me through the periods of drought and dormancy, without you, my books would not be as full and rich. There are not enough bushel baskets in the world to hold my appreciation.

And finally, I owe a huge debt to my SCBWI Regional Team, ARA Tanja Bauerle and IC Michael Hale, and the members of our Regional Planning Committee, Dianne White, Laura Ellen, Todd Gordon, and Sara Fujimura. Being able to share our writing and illustrating journeys, and the support and encouragement we provide for one another, helps keep my head in the game, especially during my dry spells.

--S.A. Skinner

ABOUT THE AUTHOR

Photo Credit: Geekssociated Press

SHARON SKINNER grew up in a small town in northern California where she spent her time reading books, making up plays and choreographing her own musicals (when she wasn't busy climbing trees and playing baseball.) She's been writing stories since the fourth grade, filling page after page with fantastical creatures, aliens, monsters and, of course, heroes.

Still a voracious and eclectic reader, Sharon also loves drawing, arts and crafts, sewing, and costume-making (especially steampunk). Her guiltiest pleasure is online gaming, and her biggest weakness is home-made, double-dark chocolate fudge. She lives in Arizona with her husband and three annoying but lovable cats.

You can find her online at sharonskinner.com

ABOUT THE ILLUSTRATOR

Photo Credit: Kyry Tek

KYNA TEK was born at a refugee camp in Thailand during the eighties and relocated to Phoenix, Arizona at the age of one. He is the Golden Brush Award winner for *Illustrators of the Future*, Volume 34. His artwork is influenced by a blend of his fascination with dark fantasy tales and admiration of video game design and aesthetics.

You can find more of his fabulous artwork at kyteki.com